Praise for *Unraveling Isobel*

"Super sexy, and so very hilarious." — *Lisa McMann*, bestselling author of the Wake trilogy

"Ideal for readers who like their stories supernatural but their dream guys human."
— *The Bulletin*

"Spine-tingling setting. . . . Isobel's sass and her steamy romance . . . will help readers race toward the dramatic conclusion." — *Publishers Weekly*

"Isobel, all snark and sharp edges covering some intense vulnerability as she continuously checks in to see if she has crossed into mental illness (as her father did when she was young), is a compelling narrator." — *Horn Book*

"This blend of paranormal romance, murder mystery, and quirky coming-of-age narrative offers tasty moments. . . . Cook gives readers a fast-paced plot, a likable narrator, and interesting characters." — *Kirkus*

"[Isobel] will quickly endear herself to readers. Cook combines the perfect mix of mystery and romance to create a delightfully creepy chick lit-y ghost story that will hook readers and keep them engrossed long into the night — preferably with the lights on." — *SLJ*

"A wonderfully creepy mystery. . . . Snarky, funny. . . . Will keep readers up late into the night. . . . Exceptional." — *Shelf Awareness*

"Filled with wit and humor, *Unraveling Isobel* draws readers in not only with romance and intrigue, but also the compelling voice of a strong protagonist. . . . Isobel makes for a complex and interesting heroine, with readers certain to root for her until the very end of this simple but well-crafted mystery." — *Voya*

Also by

EILEEN COOK

What Would Emma Do?

Getting Revenge on Lauren Wood

The Education of Hailey Kendrick

Used to Be

The Almost Truth

unraveling
isobel

EILEEN COOK

SIMON PULSE

NEW YORK   LONDON   TORONTO   SYDNEY   NEW DELHI

SIMON PULSE
An imprint of Simon & Schuster Children's Publishing Division
First Simon Pulse paperback edition October 2012
Copyright © 2012 by Eileen Cook
For information about special discounts for bulk purchases,
please contact Simon & Schuster Special Sales at 1-866-506-1949
or business@simonandschuster.com.
The Simon & Schuster Speakers Bureau can bring authors to your live event.
For more information or to book an event contact the Simon & Schuster Speakers
Bureau at 1-866-248-3049 or visit our website at www.simonspeakers.com.
Designed by Bob Steimle and Karina Granda
The text of this book was set in Adobe Garamond.
Manufactured in the United States of America
2 4 6 8 10 9 7 5 3 1
The Library of Congress has cataloged the hardcover edition as follows:
Cook, Eileen.
Unraveling Isobel / Eileen Cook.—1st Simon Pulse hardcover ed.
p. cm.
Summary: When seventeen-year-old Isobel's mother marries a man she just met
and they move to his gothic mansion on an island, strange occurrences cause Isobel
to fear that she is losing her sanity as her artist father did.
[1. Stepfamilies—Fiction. 2. Moving, Household—Fiction. 3. Ghosts—Fiction.
4. Remarriage—Fiction. 5. Islands—Washington (State)—Fiction.
6. Washington (State)—Fiction.] I. Title.
PZ7.C76955Unr 2012 [Fic]—dc23 2011032965
ISBN 978-1-4424-1327-6 (hardcover : alk. paper)
ISBN 978-1-4424-1328-3 (pbk)
ISBN 978-1-4424-1329-0 (eBook)

To Bob, who gives me reason to believe

Chapter 1

When the minister asked if anyone knew any reason why these two shouldn't be married, I should have said something. I could think of at least five reasons off the top of my head why my mom shouldn't have married Richard Wickham.

1. His name is Richard, which is really just a fancy version of Dick. I don't think anyone should be in a relationship with a Dick.

2. My mom met Richard (Dick) three months ago on the internet. If I wanted to go to a movie with a guy I met on the computer, I would get a lecture about creeps who lurk online. Not to mention, when you can measure your dating history in weeks (twelve!), then you have no business getting married.

3. Dick has a son my age, Nathaniel, who happens to be unbelievably good-looking and is now officially off-limits because we're related.

4. Just because my mom wanted to be married, I have to go along for the ride. I'm being forced to move my senior year from Seattle to an island where there are more endangered birds than there are people.

5. Dick's first wife and daughter died seven months ago, and it seems to me he could have given it at least a year before bringing us in as the replacements. I may not be the queen of etiquette, but even I know some things are in bad taste.

As the ferry chugged closer to Nairne Island, suddenly I noticed reason number six looming over me.

"Well, there she is," Dick said in a booming voice. He sounded like an actor on a stage waiting for those around him to burst into spontaneous applause at his mere presence. "What do you think of your new home, Isobel?" He gave my back a hearty slap that nearly knocked me to the deck.

I looked at my mom for confirmation. I hoped it was a joke, but instead of laughing, she was looking at Dick like a slice of chocolate cheesecake after an extended sugar-free diet. She'd said the house was big and that it had been in Dick's family since the late 1800s when his family established a town on the island. However, she'd neglected to mention that it wasn't big; it was *huge*. Most hotels are smaller than this house. It sat on the top of the tip of the island like a fat brick lady squatting down to get a good look at what was coming in and out of the harbor. The center of the house had a row of large arched windows with a stone terrace in front. The wings on both sides were covered in ivy. Not in a nice Big Ten–campus sort of way, but more like a wild-jungle-vine-gone-rabid kind of way.

"What's that style called? Early Ostentatious?"

"Isobel!" my mom said, shooting me the look that meant *Boy, are you in for it when we're alone.*

Dick gave one of his hearty "yo-ho-ho, I'm Lord of the Manor" laughs. "Now, don't be mad at her. Seeing Morrigan for the first time can be a bit overwhelming."

My eyebrows went up. "Morrigan? You gave your house a name?" I bet Richard was the kind of guy who names everything, including his car, his favorite golf club, his dick. Dick's dick. I shuddered. That was the kind of image that could leave some serious emotional scars.

"Most estates have names," Dick said, subtly pointing out that while normal people live in houses, this was an *estate*. Like I needed a reminder. Our old two-bedroom bungalow would most likely fit in the foyer of this place.

"I'm sure Morrigan will feel like home for us in no time," my mom said.

Nathaniel snorted, and the three of us looked at him. My new stepbrother was good-looking, but his mood was a downer. The phrase "turn that frown upside down" didn't seem to be his personal motto. It wasn't clear to me if this was part of his personality, or if he was just unhappy with my mom and me as the recent additions to the family. He stood apart from us with his hands jammed into his pockets, and his expression looked like he smelled something nasty. It wasn't me. I'd had a long shower that morning, and knowing this day wasn't going to be an easy one, I'd applied enough deodorant to keep an Olympic swimmer dry. There was no reason for him to always try to stand a few steps away from me. At least no reason I could figure out.

"What did you mean by that?" his dad asked. Nathaniel shrugged. Dick opened his mouth to say something else, but Nathaniel was already turning away and heading back inside the ferry's main cabin. My mom put a hand on Dick's arm and they shared a look, which I could tell meant *Kids . . . what are you going to do? No one will adopt them at this age.* I would have snorted too and followed Nathaniel inside except for the fact that apparently he couldn't stand me.

"I should get our things together. We'll be docking in a few minutes," Dick said, patting my mom's ass. I turned around and looked back at the island so I could miss their parting kiss. I knew they would kiss as if he were heading off to war instead of leaving for ten minutes to go get the car.

My mom stood next to me after Dick left. Her hands gripped

the metal railing as if she planned to vault up and over. Of course, with her wedding ring on she would sink to the bottom of the ocean in record time. The ring Dick gave her is so large it practically requires its own zip code.

"You could make this easier," she said.

"So could you."

"We're not talking about this again. You can't live with Anita." My mom had dismissed the perfectly rational idea of me living with my best friend as if I had instead suggested that I live on the streets in an old washing-machine box.

"Why not?" I couldn't help pleading again. "Her mom's fine with it." I twisted the ring on my finger and added in a softer voice, "It's my senior year."

"All the more reason I want you to be with me. You'll be leaving for college after this." She tucked a strand of hair behind my ear. "Honestly, Isobel, you don't have to act like it's a prison term. As you keep pointing out, it's just one year."

I knew it was a lost cause, but I couldn't help expressing my misery anyway. "If it's just one year, then maybe you could have waited to marry Sir Dick."

"His name is Richard, and drop the 'sir' stuff."

"Are you telling me you don't notice that he does it? The whole fake British accent thing?" There was no way she could be that oblivious.

"Isobel, don't push it. I know you're not happy about this, but someday you'll understand."

"I don't want to understand later. I want to understand now." I knew I was pushing it, but I couldn't stop myself. "Why couldn't we all live in Seattle for the year?"

"Because Richard's life is here."

I felt my throat tighten. "What about *our* life?"

"In case you didn't notice, we didn't have much of a life." My mom spun and stalked off.

I sighed, and it was lost in the wind. The ferry whistle blew as we pulled into the dock. The boat bounced off the giant wooden pylons as it came to rest, and I grabbed the railing to keep my balance. The tide was out in the harbor; the water had peeled back, leaving a graveyard of crushed oyster shells and slick seaweed. Two seagulls were fighting over a piece of some nasty dead bit they had pulled from an oyster shell. The sour smell of dead fish and rotting seaweed washed over me.

Home sweet home.

Chapter 2

We were setting new records for family dysfunction. It was only a few hours after the wedding and already Mom and Dick weren't talking. When he drove off the ferry, Dick asked my mom if there was enough room on her side of the car for him to clear the metal gate. I could have told him this was a bad plan, as my mom has zero skills in the spatial-relations area. Of course she said yes, and the next thing you know Dick had a four-inch scrape on the side of his Mercedes. He was pissed. My mom was pissed that he was pissed, because she felt like his car's paint finish shouldn't be more important than her feelings, blah blah blah. The honeymoon was over. I bet they were wishing they had done some time in Cancún instead of rushing back here so Nathaniel and I could start school.

Nathaniel and I didn't fight. That would have required us

to have an actual conversation. Since we met for the first time over an awkward dinner a month ago when our parents had announced their engagement, we had exchanged about ten words in total. I felt like pointing out to him that none of this was my idea either. While he might not have been that crazy about us moving in, at least *he* didn't have to leave all his friends and his life behind right before his senior year. While both of us felt screwed over by our respective parent, in my opinion, he was still less screwed than me. However, he didn't seem like a glass half full kind of guy, so I didn't bother to point this out.

Nathaniel sat as far away from me in the backseat as possible and stared out the window without saying anything. I sat as close as I could to my own window. The only sound in the car was Dick grinding a few layers of enamel off his teeth. One big, happy, blended family.

We turned off the main road and slipped through Morrigan's tall, black wrought-iron gates. The driveway was gravel and in real risk of disappearing under the encroaching trees and bushes. The tips of a few of the branches slid along the sides of the car as we drove past. This place was in desperate need of a serious weed whacking. The driveway went on forever. I hoped I wasn't going to be expected to walk down to the end of it every day and pick up the mail. I'd have to bring a compass to make sure I made it back.

"This used to be an orchard when my grandparents owned the estate," Dick said, waving out the window at a section that looked like an evil forest of twisted trees. I wouldn't have been shocked to see a troll lurking under a bush. "It's gone wild in the past few decades. I plan to bring it back to its former glory one of these days."

It looked to me like the only plan that made any sense was to burn the whole thing down and start over. I kept that thought to myself. The sickly sweet stink of fruit rotting on the ground made my stomach turn.

"I see some apples," my mom said, spinning around to look closer at the trees. "I'll have to come down here and pick them. We could make a pie."

Dick patted my mom's knee. One mention of pie and their fight seemed to be over. I didn't break it to him that my mom couldn't bake anything that didn't come out of a box. Ever since she met Dick she had started to remake herself into the ultimate happy homemaker. She talked about taking up knitting and making her own jam. I could tell she was fantasizing about wandering down to the orchard with a floppy straw gardening hat and a basket over one arm. My mom is like a kid who never outgrew her imaginary world. Only instead of imaginary friends, my mom has an imaginary life.

As long as I can remember, my mom has talked about how things would have turned out if my dad hadn't ruined everything. She married my dad with the idea that they were going to be a part of Seattle's top society. They'd had a deal: she would be the pretty one, throw all the right kinds of parties, and keep the ultimate house, and my dad would earn buckets of money in advertising.

Things were all going according to plan until my dad went crazy. Not just "oh, he's a crazy guy" kind of crazy. My dad went full-on hearing-voices, lock-him-up, heavy-meds-and-a-padded-room kind of crazy. "Psychotic break" is the term. I don't remember any of it. I was only four when it happened. Eventually my dad's mental state was stabilized with medication, but by then he was off the fast track and even farther off the family track. He decided he wanted to make real art instead of creating dancing toilet-paper characters to push tissue. He left us and moved to Portland. Now he lives in someone's converted garage, where he paints all day. My mom was left with a toddler, a pile of debt, a dead-end job as a secretary for a law firm, and a serious case of bitterness. We weren't poor, but we were a lot closer to food stamps than to trust funds. Dick was her second chance at her dream life. She wasn't letting go, even if it meant ruining my life—or if not my whole life, at the very least my senior year.

The car snaked around the final curve, and there was the house. We piled out and stared up at it. Dick stood there with his hands on his hips, looking as proud as if he had built the whole thing himself. I had to admit, the place was impressive. If the entire cast of a Jane Austen movie suddenly burst out the front door, it wouldn't have surprised me. The house looked like it had been transported directly out of the English countryside and plunked down on the island.

"Isn't it stunning?" my mom gushed, turning to me.

"I should warn you, this house is my mistress. She takes up a lot of time," Richard said, pulling Mom close.

Nathaniel and I rolled our eyes in tandem. When we caught each other doing the same thing, we both looked away quickly.

"As long as this house is your *only* mistress, we'll be just fine." Mom linked arms with Dick. I fought down my gag reflex.

"The west wing of the house is closed up." Dick pointed to one side of the house. His eyebrows drew together in concern. "It needs a few repairs."

I looked closer at the one side of the house. There were shingles missing on the roof and a few of the upstairs windows looked as if they had been boarded up from the inside. Here and there an occasional brick had broken free of the facade like a missing tooth. A few repairs? No wonder Dick and my mom got along: they both lived in fantasyland.

"The roof has a tiny leak, and the wiring is a bit old," Dick explained. "Of course, most rooms on that side aren't needed for daily use—the ballroom, the library, the gallery . . . that type of thing. It's been closed up for years, but not any longer. In the spring we'll open it up and get started on some repairs. You girls deserve the best." Mom beamed and nodded along as if the idea of renovations excited her. "There are plenty of bedrooms in the east wing. Isobel can have her choice."

Dick looked at me like he expected me to fall to my knees and thank him for not requiring me to sleep on a dingy mat in the kitchen. If I could really have any bedroom of my choice, I would choose my old room back in Seattle. He wasn't doing me any favors. I hadn't even been allowed to bring any of my own furniture, because Dick's place was full of family heirlooms that his great-great-grandfather had chiseled down from trees planted by some other long-dead relative. My mom sold most of our stuff at a garage sale. The U-Haul trailer we'd brought contained nothing more than our clothes, my art supplies, and a few knickknacks my mom wanted to keep that used to belong to my grandparents. I'd seen people go on vacation with more stuff than we had with us.

"Honey, how about that? A library in the house!" Mom turned to Dick. "She's such a bookworm. I don't know who she gets that from, because it certainly isn't me."

He gave her nose an affectionate tap with his finger. "It would be a tragedy for you to hide your pretty face in a book."

My mom laughed and squeezed Dick's arm. I noticed no one mentioned that it would be a tragedy if I kept *my* face in a book.

Dick bent over and swept my mom off her feet, and she let out a high-pitched giggle. "Nathaniel, bring in the luggage. I'm going to carry this fine woman over the threshold and make this marriage official."

Nathaniel and I stood in the driveway and watched our parents acting like idiots. There is something especially gross about knowing your parents have sex. Especially if you have no sex life of your own. I peeked over at Nathaniel. His face was made up of strong lines, like someone drew him with a ruler. He wore his hair just a bit too long, and he was always pushing it out of his face. I couldn't help but notice he had these amazing lashes models could only achieve with multiple applications of plumping mascara. I stuffed my hands in my pockets and tried to think of something to say that didn't involve either of our parents, the weather, or weddings. Nothing came to mind.

Without a word, Nathaniel started to unpack the U-Haul trailer. Before now I hadn't noticed how cheap and shabby our luggage was. The large roller bag had a piece of duct tape holding the side together, and there was a huge ink stain on my duffel bag where a pen had exploded in a pocket years ago. I felt myself flush and made a grab for my bag as soon as he unloaded it.

"I'll get it," Nathaniel said.

"I can carry my own stuff," I insisted. "Seriously, I'm not handicapped." As soon as the words flew out of my mouth, I winced. Nathaniel's younger sister had been mentally disabled. *Super,* I chided myself. *Insult his dead handicapped sister. Great way to win him over.*

"Fine." His mouth set into a firm line.

"Sorry. That didn't come out the way I wanted."

"Whatever." Nathaniel tossed a few more of our bags out of the U-Haul and onto the driveway. He paused, looking over at me. "How do you see with all that black crap all over your eyes?"

I raised my hand and touched the corner of my eye. Who did he think he was? The makeup police?

"How do you see with your head shoved so far up your ass?" I fired back and twirled around before he could say anything else. I stomped toward the house. It would have been a really dramatic exit except for the fact that the driveway was covered in at least six inches of gravel and my right foot slid out from under me. I went down hard on one knee. I heard Nathaniel start to laugh before he managed to choke it back down. I pulled myself up. My knee was bleeding.

"You okay?" Nathaniel asked.

"No. Actually, I'm not okay, and if possible, could we skip the whole part where you act like you care?" I dusted myself off and glared back at him.

Nathaniel stood with his mouth slightly open. "Whatever you want."

"If I got what I wanted, I wouldn't be here." I shouldered my bag and climbed up the front stairs.

Home sweet home. Yeah, right.

Chapter 3

The entrance hall was designed to impress. The floor was a buttery cream-colored marble and the walls were paneled in dark wood. I'm not a lumberjack, so I had no idea what kind of wood it was, but it looked expensive and it had been carved into elaborate scrolls and designs. A huge staircase dominated the room. It looked like it had been stolen from the movie set for *Gone with the Wind* or *Titanic*. At the bottom of the stairs, at either side of the railings, were two carved women holding aloft what I think were supposed to be the lamps of knowledge. The house smelled like lemon furniture polish and old books. All that was missing was an English butler named Jeeves to take my coat and bag. Impressive, but no one was going to call this place cozy.

I dragged my duffel up the main staircase. I really hoped Dick didn't think part of our "one big, happy family" plan included me cleaning this place. The main banister had been polished, but I could see some cobwebs near the ceiling. Dusting would be a full-time job in this place.

I dropped my bag at the top of the stairs and started peeking in the various rooms, looking for one I could tolerate. The bedrooms on the second floor were decorated in a style I would call uptight fussy meets grandma's house. The curtains had giant flouncy ruffles. Each of the beds came with a herd of small pillows in flowered fabrics. They looked hard and uncomfortable. A lot of the furniture seemed to be perched on tiny fragile wooden legs designed to break. A few of the rooms had wallpaper that could be used as a torture device. I was fairly certain constant exposure to those patterns could lead to blindness or insanity.

As soon as I opened the next door, I knew I'd found Nathaniel's room. The lack of floral wallpaper was a giveaway, along with a giant bag of sports gear that was spilling out onto the floor. Instead of shutting the door, I took a few steps inside after shooting a look over my shoulder to make sure he wasn't coming up the stairs. He wasn't a slob, other than the duffel bag on the floor. There weren't piles of laundry in the corners. Unlike Anita's brother's room, which always smelled like old socks, his smelled a bit like campfire smoke mixed with vanilla. There were no posters of bands or half-naked women draped over cars on his walls, instead he had a bunch of framed black-

and-white photographs. I wandered around the room touching the odd thing here and there. I wasn't sure what I was looking for—maybe something that would help me understand him. I ran my fingers over the stacks of things on his desk: a pile of loose change, a pen with a chewed cap, his music player, a stack of books for school.

There was a small frame on top of his dresser. I picked it up. A woman stood on the beach looking at the camera, shielding her eyes from the sun with one hand. Her other arm was draped around a little girl. There was an elaborate sandcastle in front of them, the sides decorated with shells and rocks. It had to be a photo of his mom and sister. It struck me that when this picture was taken, they had no idea they were going to die. I put the frame down. I didn't want to see their smiling faces. They probably thought their biggest problem was that the tide would come in and destroy the castle they spent hours making. I heard a noise in the hall and my heart sped up. I could only imagine what Nathaniel would say if he found me in his room. I backed out quickly and shut the door.

There was another room stuffed with antiques, and the next had to be the master bedroom. The room was large, but all the dark colors and heavy fabrics made the room feel claustrophobic to me. Above the dresser was a giant painting of a woman I was pretty sure was Dick's mom. The idea that he wanted a life-size portrait of his mom in his room was creepy. The windows were covered in thick red velvet draperies, and in the center of the room was a giant four-poster bed. The idea of my mom and Dick rolling around on that football-field-size mattress while his mom watched made my stomach clench. The idea of Dick in general made me nauseated.

I stood back out in the hallway. I was out of bedrooms. I wondered if it would be rude to ask Dick if he was open to some major remodeling. I'm not a giant pink cabbage-rose-bedroom kind of person. I was trying to picture Dick's face if I used pushpins on his walls to hang up my poster of Klimt's painting *The Kiss*. Then I noticed the door. It was covered in the same paneling as the wall, and the handle was a small brass knob designed to blend in to the wood detailing. I must have walked right past it. I'd barely touched the handle when the door clicked open to reveal a narrow staircase leading up. I was surprised. From the outside, it hadn't looked like the house had a third floor.

At the top of the stairs there were two more doors. I opened one and found the attic. It ran the length of the wing. The ceiling was sloped, giving the room the appearance of a huge wooden tent. The room was dusty, with piles of old leather trunks that looked like they were last used in the 1800s when the Wickham family moved in. I wandered in farther. I pulled a sheet off one of the giant lumps to expose a rack of dresses. They were ball gowns. My hands ran down the sides of an emerald-green silk dress. The bodice was covered in blue, green, and gray beads. There was a handwritten dry cleaning tag on the hanger. Elizabeth Wickham.

That was Dick's mom. Apparently, she didn't just keep her house like a royal estate, she liked to dress as if she were a queen too. The dress was stunning in a cool vintage over-the-top way, but since I was hardly ever (as in never) invited to royal balls, I hadn't a clue where I would wear it. Across the aisle I spotted a row of boxes marked TOYS. A lonely stuffed zebra sat on top of one box. One of his eyes was gone, and someone had sewn a black button on in its place.

"Tragic war injury?" I asked, picking him up. I expected the zebra to smell musty, but he smelled clean and almost minty, like toothpaste, maybe. I touched his button eye. "Don't you worry about it," I told him. "Real women dig men with scars. Gives them character." I tucked the floppy zebra under my arm and went back into the hall.

As soon as I opened the only other door, I knew I had found my bedroom. It was larger than the other bedrooms downstairs, but much of the space was lost, due to the ceilings that sloped down to the floor like a Parisian garret. Two big windows opened to the back of the house, each with a deep inset window seat. I kneeled in the first and peered out. The view was amazing. You could see the stone patio I had noticed from the ferry, and beyond that, the cliff edge jutting out, and then the ocean. The waves marched along in perfect formation, and I could hear the sound of them breaking against the rocks, even through the thick glass.

The floor was wide-planked hardwood that had been stained

so dark it looked nearly black. The walls were a soft gray instead of the insipid pinks of downstairs. There wasn't a single inch of ugly wallpaper or giant floral fabric anywhere. There was another door, which led to a small bathroom. My own bathroom! I gave the zebra a hug in glee. The bed wasn't made up, but a soft white blanket had been pulled over the mattress. The only other furniture in the room was a desk tucked into one of the corners and a low bookshelf that was completely empty.

I put my duffel bag down and looked around the room. It was perfect.

"What the hell are you doing?"

I jumped when I heard the voice. Nathaniel was standing in the doorway looking at me, his eyes the same cold gray color as the ocean outside.

"Your dad told me to pick out a bedroom." I hated how my voice sounded so defensive.

"Well, you can't have this one."

"Look, if you wanted it, you should have called dibs before now. I saw yours downstairs."

"You went through my room?" He yanked up his sleeves as if he was getting ready to start a fistfight with me.

My face flushed red-hot. "I didn't 'go through' your room. I opened the door and figured it was yours since it was one of the few places that wasn't pink," I said, hoping he wouldn't call me on my lie.

"You're a girl. You're supposed to like pink."

"Tell me you did *not* just say that."

"What? Pink doesn't go with your goth image?"

"My image isn't goth," I said through clenched teeth.

"What is it then?"

"Nothing. I'm capable of coming up with my own look instead of dressing like a clone."

"Dressing all in black is being a rebel clone. Low rent."

"Fuck you."

"Isobel!" My mom and Dick appeared in the doorway. My mom's face was flushed. I had the sense she wasn't impressed with my language choice.

"Did you hear what he said to me?" I asked her.

"No, and we don't want to know." Dick crossed his arms and gave both Nathaniel and me a stern look. "We're not going to get in the middle of you two. Do you think we can't see what you're doing? We're a family now. You can't ask your mom to take your side any more than Nathaniel can expect me to take his. The two of you are going to have to work things out on your own, and I would hope that you could learn to do it without resorting to foul language."

"But she—" Nathaniel started to say.

"Nathaniel, remember your breeding," Dick barked. Nathaniel swallowed whatever he was about to say and stood up straight as if he were in a military prep school. "Honestly, you two are acting like children."

"She wants this as her bedroom," Nathaniel said, biting off

each word. "I was trying to explain to her that wasn't possible."

I wasn't backing down. "You said I could pick out whatever bedroom I wanted. No one is using this room, so what's the big deal?" This was the room I wanted. Not only was it the only room I could possibly imagine myself living in for the next year, it was also separate from the rest of the house. I needed some distance if I was going to survive.

"How did you even get up here?" Nathaniel asked. "The door to this floor is kept locked."

"It wasn't locked," I said.

"It's always locked."

"Okay, you busted me. I jimmied the lock, just a little trick I learned on the wrong side of the tracks with my low-rent buddies."

"Isobel, honestly. What has gotten into you?" My mom shook her head as if she didn't know me.

"The door wasn't locked," I repeated.

"This was my sister's room," Nathaniel said.

The air was suddenly sucked out of the space. My mom looked at me as if she blamed me for bringing up this awkward issue. How was I supposed to know this was Evelyn's room? It wasn't as if there was a nameplate on the door, and there wasn't a thing left on the walls or shelf that would indicate it belonged to anyone. Besides, why would her bedroom have been so far away from the others? I suddenly remembered the stuffed zebra. Shit. I bet that belonged to Evelyn too. The zebra was propped up next to the duffel bag at my feet. It didn't look like anyone had seen him yet. With a silent apology, I nudged him under the bed with my foot so he was out of sight. I didn't need to be accused of poaching the dead girl's toys in addition to her room.

"If Isobel wants this room, it should be hers," Dick said. I couldn't tell who was most surprised by his announcement.

"Dad!" Nathaniel looked shocked. I could tell he had expected his dad to back him up on this one.

"She can pick something else," my mom rushed in to say. "She doesn't need to be a bother."

"We can't keep this room a shrine to the past." Dick gave a weak smile. "I should have realized a girl would want her own bathroom and some space to herself. You go ahead and move your things up here."

"Seriously?" I asked.

"This was Evie's room," Nathaniel said again. His jaw was tight and it looked to me like his eyes were starting to tear up.

"The house is centuries old. If we saved rooms for all the people who were gone, we would have run out of rooms by now. We'd be forced to sleep in the garage." Dick chuckled, but I could tell Nathaniel didn't find the situation even remotely funny. I couldn't really blame him. His mom and sister hadn't even been gone a year and Dick was acting like it was no big deal. "Nathaniel can show you where the linens are kept, Isobel, so you can make up your bed. Now, you get settled, and your mom and I will rustle up some sandwiches for dinner. It's been a long day. Later we can play a round of Scrabble together." Dick clapped his hands like he was a kindergarten teacher and it was activity time. My mom was giving him a tearful smile like she couldn't believe how brave and caring he was being by letting me have the bedroom.

Nathaniel and I stared at each other. I wasn't sure where things had gotten so off track between us. Actually, we'd never really been *on* track. When I met him, I thought he looked rich, like when he was a baby his diapers had been cashmere. He came across as the kind of person who would never hang out with someone like me, and so far, that had proven to be the case.

"Look," I began, but before I could say another word, Nathaniel turned around and left, slamming the door behind him.

"I'll talk to him." Dick followed him out, treating the door more gently.

Now that we were alone, my mom shot me a look.

"I didn't do anything. Dick told me to pick out a bedroom."

"Would you *please* call him Richard?" My mom paced the room and then stopped to gaze out the window. "I know you're not happy, but is it asking too much that you try to make this work?"

"Mom, this is my senior year—" I began.

"This is the beginning of the rest of my life," she cut in. "Do you know how many things I put on hold for you? How much I sacrificed over the years? Now I have a chance to start over. *We* have a chance to start over. Having Richard as a stepfather is going to open doors for you, too. Can't you give me one year of your life when I've given you seventeen?"

I loved how she had this way of making my entire existence a burden to her when I hadn't asked to be born in the first place. "You don't believe me, but I'm doing the best I can. I'm here. I'm trying, but it's hard. I don't know anyone."

"You know Nathaniel."

"Nathaniel hates me," I pointed out.

"He doesn't hate you. He's just having a hard time with all of this."

"Welcome to the party."

"Nathaniel is sensitive because of what happened to his mom and sister."

"What *did* happen? Was it a car accident?" My mom had always been vague about how Dick's first wife and Evelyn had died. It didn't seem like the kind of thing I could ask a lot of questions about without coming across like an insensitive jerk. For some reason, with all the wedding planning there had never been a good time to bring up the dead first wife.

"No, it was a boating accident."

My knowledge of sailboats and yachts was pretty sketchy. All I could picture was some kind of *Titanic*-type incident, but there weren't even any icebergs out here. What else could happen to a boat? Did it run into another boat? Isn't the ocean big enough that they shouldn't run into anything else?

"Wow." I was at a loss for anything else to say. How did Nathaniel stand this house, with the sound of the ocean in the background like a constant reminder? No wonder the guy was edgy.

"Richard says Nathaniel hasn't been the same since the accident. He withdrew from his friends, quit the soccer team, and won't talk about it with Richard no matter how hard he tries. He won't even step foot on the boat."

"Dick kept the boat?" My voice came out a little screechy, and my mom raised an eyebrow. "I mean, Richard still has the boat? Isn't that weird?" By weird I meant disturbing as hell, and morbid, but I was trying to be more balanced in my communication style.

"If it were just any boat, that would be one thing, but it's a handmade wooden sailboat from the 1950s. It's been in his family a long time. Richard's dad was the one who restored it."

"Huh." Maybe Dick's dad had restored it, but his wife and daughter had *died* on it. I'm all for family memories, but this felt wrong on so many levels.

"It was an accident, after all. It wasn't like it was the boat's fault." Mom's face flushed, which told me that she thought it was creepy too, but she wasn't going to admit it. "He understands how upsetting it is, especially for Nathaniel, so he keeps it locked in the boathouse for now."

My mom started picking at her thumbnail the way she always does when she's stressed. During most of my childhood, she had raw, bloody cuticles from where she would tear the skin off. She'd stopped in the past few months. For the wedding, she'd even gotten a manicure. "I'll try harder," I said, giving in.

My mom gave me a huge smile. I could see her take a deep breath. She crossed the room with a quick stride and hugged me.

"That's all I can ask, just give it a try. Richard likes you. He's trying really hard to make you feel at home here."

I didn't bother telling her that the harder Dick tried, the more it made me want to run away. My mom brushed the hair out of my eyes and slipped out of the room. I could hear the waves outside. I sat down on the bed and pulled the zebra out from underneath.

"Looks like it's just you and me, buddy."

When you're seventeen and the only friend you have in town is a stuffed animal that doesn't even belong to you, I think it's safe to say your life is officially in the shitter.

Chapter 4

"You did *not* move into the dead girl's room!" Anita's voice screeched through my cell phone. My best friend has two volume settings—mute and screaming. She's never going to make it as a librarian, that's for sure. She has never understood the concept of using your inside voice. Then again, "moderation" isn't a term I would ever use when describing Anita.

"It's the nicest bedroom in the place." I looked around the room from my vantage point of the center of the bed. After a dinner where Dick and my mom pretended everything was fine and Nathaniel ignored me completely, I decided against an evening of board games, no matter how fun Dick tried to make it sound. Apparently his mom was some big Scrabble nut, so he wanted to carry on another fine family tradition. Most likely there was an heirloom Wickham Scrabble set with tiles some distant relative whittled out of trees that used to grow on the estate property.

Instead I went up to my room to get organized. I made the bed and hung my poster on the far wall. I stuck Mr. Stripes back under the bed so I wouldn't be accused of stuffie stealing. I unpacked a bunch of postcards of paintings that I had bought from the art museum in Seattle or had picked up at the various galleries, and made them into a collage on the wall above my bed. I piled my books onto the shelves and stuck the few other things I had brought around the room so it felt more like my own space. I stared out the window. I'd never had a room with a view before, unless you count looking directly into our neighbor's house. Mr. Turken tended to dance around in his boxers a lot. I usually kept my curtains shut. The wind was picking up now and it looked like it was going to turn into a big storm.

"I can hardly hear you," Anita yelled in my ear.

"I know, the reception here sucks. I didn't want to call you on the landline in case Dick has a rule about long-distance charges."

"Dick's a dick. Let's talk about someone more interesting. How's lover boy?"

"He's my stepbrother now, remember? Most states have laws against sleeping with a sibling."

"He's not your real brother, which means he's fair game. Totally legit. Besides, could he be better looking? It's always open season on someone that hot. If you don't want him, I'll swim over there and take him off your hands."

"He's not on my hands. He can't stand me."

"Not stand you? With all your wit and charm? He must be playing hard to get."

"More like impossible to get. Besides, he's my stepbrother. I'm hoping that somewhere on this island there will be someone who is reasonably attractive, not a weirdo, *and* not related to me."

"Negative energy! Blow it out. You want to attract positive energy. Think white-light stuff. Happy thoughts."

I suddenly missed her like crazy. "I wish I was there. This sucks."

"Just remember, by this time next year we'll be roommates." We had already vowed to apply to the University of Washington and get an apartment together near campus. "Visualize the end goal so the universe knows what you want. Besides, you're living on an island in the middle of nowhere. Think of it like an artist's retreat. People pay big money to go to those things, and you're there for free. You can get a bunch of stuff done for your portfolio without being distracted by civilization and stuff."

"My mom is still dead set against me getting a degree in art."

"You don't have to do what your mom says at that point. You'll be eighteen."

"Eighteen with about a hundred and fifty bucks to my name. I'm pretty sure college tuition is going to cost me more than that."

"That's why they have student aid, to aid students. Have faith that the universe will provide, but you have to be willing to do your part. You can't expect fate to carry the whole load.

Take steps toward your goal to show your commitment. The universe needs to know you're not screwing around. A portfolio demonstrates to the universe that you're serious. Draw some pictures, suck in all that island air and inspiration."

"That assumes living in an old, broken-down house will inspire me."

As if in protest to my statement, a burst of static blared, and I yanked the phone away from my ear. I could hear Anita call out my name, but her voice was distant. It sounded like we were talking on one of those tin can string phones.

"Anita? Can you hear me?"

The phone gave a blare of static in return. I called her name again, but the call went dead with a click and then silence. The lights flickered, and then they went out completely. A second later they were back on, but it was long enough without power to make my clock radio blink 12:00 at me.

I knew the storm outside, combined with the poor cell service, was to blame, but for an instant it felt like the house was mad I'd insulted it.

I shivered and then shook off the feeling. I checked my phone, but there was zero reception. Annoyed, I tossed the phone into my bag. Well, if I couldn't finish my conversation with Anita, at least I could take her advice. I pulled my sketchbook off the shelf and flipped through it until I found a clean page. Anita was flakey, but she was also right a lot of the time. I had my heart set on being accepted into the art program at U-Dub, which meant

I had to have a portfolio ready to show by the time I sent in my application, especially if I wanted any kind of scholarship. I was going to need some money to pay the bills, because when my mom found out I wanted to major in art, she was going to freak out. "Freak out" being an understatement.

My mom blamed my dad's passion for art for everything. She often pointed out that van Gogh cut off his own ear and you never heard of accountants doing something like that. She wasn't sure which came first, the crazy or the art, but she wasn't taking any chances with me. As far as my mom was concerned, I should go to school and study nursing or accounting. I think she thought she was being supermom for giving me a choice at all. The fact that I got a D in tenth-grade biology and couldn't stand math didn't faze her. Art was the one thing that I was really good at. Sometimes drawing felt like the only thing keeping me sane. It was like my pencil could figure things out before the rest of me.

There was no point worrying about it right now, though. I got myself settled on my bed and started sketching the room, trying to catch the angle of the walls and the deep-set windows. I smudged a pencil line with my little finger to give the corner the feeling of piled shadows. I felt my focus narrow down to the point where my pencil met the paper. The wind outside picked up speed. I got lost in the picture, trying to make it work.

Somewhere along the way, I must have fallen asleep.

That's when I saw her.

Chapter 5

I woke up to a loud bang. I sat up in bed, confused. The lights were out. For a second I didn't know where I was. I felt ungrounded, like I was floating in the darkness. The sensation made me dizzy. I put my feet down on the floor. If it worked for bed spins, it would work for this. When my feet touched the ice-cold floorboards, I was instantly alert.

Another bang.

I spun around and saw the window frame bounce against the wall. The latch must not have been secured, and the wind had blown it open. Another blast of freezing wind rushed in, and the curtain billowed out. For a second I felt a wave of relief. It was just the storm. Then there was a crack of lightning and the room lit up. And there she was.

She was young, that age between chubby baby cheeks and

gangly arms and legs. Her eyes were wide and she was staring at me. She seemed as surprised to see me as I was to see her. She was soaking wet. Her dark hair was slicked down on her head, and a piece of seaweed was glued to one cheek. She reached out, her hands opening and closing into tight fists. I yanked my feet back into bed and scrambled back until I was pressing against the headboard.

Her eyes were blank and dark, like a black marker had colored them in. She took a step forward and opened her mouth wide. I couldn't hear over my own scream if she made any noise at all. There was another crack of lightning, and then she wasn't there. I closed my eyes and screamed again.

The bedroom door crashed open and the overhead light came on. Nathaniel burst in wearing only his boxer shorts and breathing heavily. Even though I was terrified, I couldn't help but notice that Nathaniel had been hiding a nice body under his designer jeans and button-down shirts. Dick and my mom were just a few steps behind him, their bathrobes tied tight at the waist. Not that I wanted to notice, but it was also apparent that Dick looked better dressed than half undressed.

"What in the world?" Dick pushed past Nathaniel and latched the window shut.

"Are you okay?" My mom rushed to the bed and took my hand.

"There was a girl," I said.

"A girl?" My mom looked over at Dick as if she expected him to explain.

I pointed to the spot where I'd seen her. "I woke up and she was there. Just standing there."

"Sounds like someone had a bit too much cake for dessert," Dick said with a chuckle, but his mouth was turned down. "Upset stomachs make for bad dreams. Most likely the window blew open and the curtain caught your eye. Since you were half awake, you saw something that wasn't there. New house must have given you the jitters."

My mom's face registered relief, and she patted my arm reassuringly. Dick smiled as if he'd just gotten the correct answer on *Jeopardy!* I wasn't so sure. It hadn't felt like a Sara Lee–induced hallucination to me. Maybe I'd only been half awake at first, but once I touched my feet to the floor, I would have sworn I was wide awake.

Then I realized something else. "The lights were out. I didn't turn them out."

"I did," Nathaniel said. "I came up to talk to you a couple of hours ago, but you were already asleep. I pulled a blanket over you and left."

I couldn't decide if the fact that Nathaniel had watched me when I was sleeping was creepy or sort of exciting. God, I hoped I hadn't been lying there with my mouth open and drooling.

My mom noticed my sketchbook on the floor and grabbed it. "Were you drawing?" she demanded.

"It's just a sketch, Mom." She made it sound like she'd caught me rolling joints in my room or posting racy pictures of myself online. She wasn't prepared to say I wasn't allowed to draw, but she'd made it abundantly clear she would rather I take up just about any other hobby, up to and including recreational drug use. An addiction was something she could deal with, but in her opinion, art was nothing but trouble.

"I thought we talked about the fact that you need to focus on your schoolwork. Art isn't a practical or useful way to spend your time."

"You think I should spend all my free time learning physics?"

"Don't be smart with me," she warned, completely missing the irony.

"Now, now, let's not make a mountain out of a molehill," Dick said. "Everyone's tense because it's the middle of the night. If Isobel likes to tinker about with pencils, then I think it's great. She doesn't start school here until Monday, so there's plenty of time for her to crack the books later. Let's call it a night and tackle this in the morning."

I couldn't decide what was worse: that Dick was sticking up for me, or that he'd used the phrase "tinker with pencils." He took the sketchbook from my mom and flipped through the pages. I felt a millimeter of tooth enamel grind down. Sketchbooks are private. You don't just flip through someone's work unless you've been invited. Dick stopped at the last page.

He made a strange sound in the back of his throat.

"What's this?" He held out the sketchbook and shook it like there was something incriminating about it. His mouth was pressed into a tight smile, but his eyes looked flat and angry. What happened to no harm being done with pencil tinkering?

"I was just drawing the room."

His face looked like he'd discovered me doing pictures of animals in compromising positions. Dick tossed the sketchbook on the bed. I noticed then that something was wrong.

I picked up the book and took a closer look at my drawing. The room was done in strong black lines with the shadows in the corners, the way I remembered doing it, but now there were framed pictures hanging on the wall, and the shelves were stacked with kids' games, books, and stuffed animals. On the window seat at the center of the picture, my buddy the stuffed zebra leaned against a book; in the sketch, he still had both eyes. It was the same room, but from a different time, when it was someone else's room.

"I didn't do that," I said. My mom raised one eyebrow and picked my hand up out of my lap, displaying the dark graphite still smudged on my fingers. "No, I mean, I drew part of the picture, but not all of it," I tried to explain.

"If you didn't draw it, who did? Your imaginary friend?" My mom shook her head, unable to meet my eyes. "This is why you should leave the art to someone else."

I felt my throat close tight. I refused to cry. She made it sound like the fact that I had been drawing something was connected to the fact I'd seen something, as if, had I read a book instead, I never would have had a nightmare.

"Let me see." Nathaniel stepped forward to take the sketchbook from my bed. Dick snatched it back before he could reach it. Before I knew what was happening, Dick had torn the page free and ripped it in two. Even my mom looked surprised. Dick folded the scraps of paper in half and tore them again.

"If you didn't draw the picture, then you won't miss it," Dick said with a smile. He dropped the scraps into the trash can, where they fluttered to the bottom like broken butterflies. I stared at Dick, wondering if he'd lost his mind. "There's no sense in getting everyone riled up over something silly like a picture. Now there won't be any more nightmares." Dick patted my shoulder like he was getting ready to tuck me in. He smiled at my mom. "Now, don't you get riled up either. She wouldn't be a normal teenager if she wasn't doing something to upset you."

"I think we've had enough excitement for one day," my mom said. She took Dick's hand and they left. I knew once they got back to their bedroom she was going to talk to him about how important it was to have a united front against my art. It made me want to scream.

But I couldn't. Nathaniel was still standing there awkwardly, looking as though he had just realized we were alone and that he was only wearing boxers. I could tell Nathaniel was one of those people who liked to be in control, and being stranded half naked in my room wasn't exactly in his comfort zone. I couldn't help enjoying the moment. It was nice to have him as the one who felt out of place for a change.

"Why did you come up to my room?" I asked.

"You were screaming."

"I meant before, when you turned out the lights."

"I came up to apologize." He crossed his arms over his chest. "I was out of line earlier. Being mad at you for any of this doesn't make sense."

I hadn't been sure what he was going to say, but I hadn't been expecting an apology.

"It's okay. It's a weird situation."

"Did you . . ." Nathaniel broke off what he was going to say. He chewed on his lower lip while he looked out the window. It was unbelievably sexy.

God, I would kill for him to chew on my lower lip like that. Yeah, right. That was about as likely as my mom gushing over my artwork. Still, I couldn't help admiring the muscles in his arms and chest while he was temporarily preoccupied. He was definitely hot enough to be a model, and the brooding look on his face didn't hurt a bit. I wondered what he was thinking about, staring off into the rainy night like that.

"Did I what?" I prompted.

He looked back at me as if he was surprised to see I was still there. Somehow, I doubted he'd been lost in a lip nibbling fantasy.

"Never mind. Good night." He slipped out the doorway, and I could hear his bare feet slapping against the wooden stairs.

I was alone again.

Well, not completely alone. I still had Mr. Stripes, everyone's favorite zebra. He was sitting on the window seat, sort of flopped over like he was also exhausted by the events of the day.

I sat up straight. The last time I had seen Mr. Stripes was when I'd put him under the bed. What was he doing on the window seat? I swallowed and then leaned over slowly. I took a deep breath and yanked up the bed skirt. Nothing. Just a couple of dust bunnies. I must have moved him before I fell asleep. I looked back over at the zebra.

"Mr. Stripes?" The zebra just lay there. He didn't look like the kind of stuffed animal that would move across the room by himself. But then I remembered the picture.

I crossed the room and fished the scraps of the drawing out of the trash. I assembled them like puzzle pieces on the desktop until they were back in order. It was as I remembered it, Mr. Stripes in the same position on the window seat. Only in the picture he was leaning on a book. I looked around slowly. If the book suddenly appeared, I was fully prepared to leave the house and sleep in the car. I'd had enough of things popping up out of the ether. Nothing. Just Mr. Stripes. It didn't look like he had moved. I must have propped him up for the picture and forgotten about it. I must have been imagining how the room had looked when Evelyn had lived in it, and then I must have drawn it, fallen asleep, and had a nightmare. That had to be it. There wasn't any other explanation, was there? No rational reason.

My heart was pounding. There was another option, one I didn't want to consider at all, even though it kept tickling at the back of my brain. Why couldn't I remember drawing the picture? I took after my dad in terms of art ability, but I was really hoping to avoid taking after him in the mental health area. Schizophrenia was thought to have a genetic component. It was one of those things that my mom and I never discussed, but there were times when I would catch her watching me. Evaluating. Was I being too emotional? Paranoid? Was I going to snap like he did? No wonder I tended to go from having a nightmare like any other normal person to assuming I had actually seen something. Everyone has nightmares. There's nothing odd about being freaked out when you first wake up.

I brushed the pieces of the picture back into the trash and then, for some reason, fished them back out. I shuffled them into a stack and stuck them in the back of one of my old Harry Potter books. I licked my finger and wiped the graphite dust off on my yoga pants. And Nathaniel thought I wore a lot of black because I was making a statement. Little did he know that it covered up for my tendency to be a slob.

It was dark out. I couldn't see anything, but I could still hear the waves. I decided to check the latch again just to be safe. I stepped into a cold puddle of water and jumped back, startled. I bent down and trailed a finger through the water. The wind must have blown some of the rain in. I touched my finger to my lips. The water was salty. Ocean water. My heart sped up. Rainwater isn't salty, is it? I touched the water again and felt something slick. I held up my hand. A tiny sliver of seaweed hung down from my index finger.

I slept with the bedside light on.

Chapter 6

Everything seemed different in the morning. Safer, more grounded. When I got up the house was silent. I looked out at the water and the blue sky. My fear from last night now seemed way out of proportion. I'd had a nightmare, nothing more. I hated to admit Dick might be right, but in this case he was. It had been a big day—the wedding, moving to the house, fighting with Nathaniel over the room. I woke up with the storm going on, saw the curtain blowing in the wind, and my brain filled in the rest. As for the puddle of water, it had dried up. Either I imagined the salty taste, or the fact that we lived next to the ocean made the rainwater salty. What was I, a meteorologist? How was I supposed to know what the rain tasted like out here? I took a deep breath and gave the window lock another shake proving to myself it was latched tight.

I wandered downstairs. There was a note in the kitchen from my mom. She and Dick had gone into town for groceries. I was willing to bet that when Dick went back to work, this whole "doing everything side by side as if he and my mom were Noah's-ark creatures" would stop. Dick struck me as the kind of guy who expected a cold martini and warm slippers waiting for him when he got home. Of course, he worked from home, so he wouldn't have far to go to keep an eye on my mom and make sure she was doing what he wanted. I looked around the counter. There wasn't any note from Nathaniel, not that I expected him to hang around and show me the place just because he had thawed out enough that we could have an actual conversation.

The kitchen was large and looked like it had last been updated around 1920. There wasn't even a dishwasher, and the stove was this huge metal behemoth. I would not have been shocked if someone told me it required coal. I rummaged around and found a bagel in the bread drawer and decided to eat it cold rather than bother trying to find a toaster. With my luck, this place didn't even have a toaster and I'd be expected to hold the bagel over an open flame in a fireplace or something.

I walked over to the pantry while I nibbled on the bagel. The wood on the door was grooved with notches, and names and dates had been carved into it. My fingers ran over the scars in the wood. The dates went back to the 1940s. I found one for Nathaniel. It looked like he had gotten tall at a young age.

There were a few grooves for Evelyn as well. I ran my finger over one of her notches.

I thought about going back up to my room, but since I had the house to myself, it was a perfect opportunity to do a bit of exploring in my new home. I skated around the wood floors in my socks.

We lived in the east wing. The main floor had the kitchen, a dining room that could comfortably seat twenty or so of my closest friends (assuming I could even come up with twenty people I wanted to hang out with), and what I guessed was a formal living room. The way the furniture looked completely unsuitable for actual use was the giveaway to the formal part. Based on the artwork hanging on the walls, it didn't look like the Wickham family was into modern stuff. Most of the paintings were either portraits (no doubt of long-dead illustrious Wickhams) or sea scenes.

Just past the formal living room was a slightly less formal family room. At least the sofa wasn't as hard as granite and there was a TV. I clicked the TV on and ran through the channels. The house had cable, thank God. I turned it off and continued exploring. Off the family room were glass French doors that were locked. Interesting. People should realize locking stuff up only makes it more intriguing. I peered in. It looked like it must be Dick's study. It was heavy on the man decor, including a couple of severed animal heads hanging on the wall. No doubt some Wickham had hunted them down and killed them while on safari with Hemingway or something. I could see that the moose head was covered in a thick felt of gray dust. Something scurried about in the open mouth of a bear. It was a huge spider. Nasty. A modern flat-screen computer looked out of place on the desk.

Then I heard it. A high, tinkling laugh. A little girl's laugh. The bit of bagel I'd just bitten off froze in my throat. I took a few tentative steps down the hall. I heard it again coming from the last room. I stood outside the door and made myself count to five, doing the yoga breathing that Anita was always trying to teach me. I hadn't heard anything; it was just the wind in the trees or something. Then the laugh came again. I went from Zen to freak-out in .002 seconds. My hand clenched down on the doorknob.

"Who is that?" My voice came out shaky and thin, which hadn't been what I was going for. I had the sense it was better to come across as in charge when dealing with the undead, or the next thing you know they'd be haunting you like they owned the place. I cleared my throat and tried again, this time more firmly. "Who are you?"

The laugh carried through the door again.

"I mean you no harm." I waited, but there was no response. Maybe she was waiting for more details. "Are you not at peace?" As soon as the words left my mouth I felt like kicking myself. Of course she wasn't at peace. She died in a tragic accident at a young age, and now someone had taken over her room, not to mention her stuffed zebra. She was a ghost with a lot of issues. You don't hear about ghosts at peace wandering around. Haunting is strictly an occupation for seriously unpeaceful dead people.

I took another deep breath and flung the door open. It bounced against the far wall and then swung back, shutting in my face. One thing was becoming clear: if I was thinking of becoming an international ghost hunter, I was going to need some remedial training. I opened the door again, this time with a bit less vim and vigor.

"Show yourself," I commanded.

It was a sunroom. The floors were slate tiles and there were floor-to-ceiling glass windows looking out onto the patio. The furniture was wicker with white cushions that looked past their prime, turning yellow. The room smelled vaguely of mildew, like damp towels forgotten in a washing machine. I had the sense that this had been a room Dick's first wife had liked. Since she was gone, it seemed no one used it.

Then I heard the laugh again. I whirled around, ready to confront the ghost. Right outside the window was a wind chime, some type of sea glass and shell thing. That was what had made the sound. Fantastic. I had been attempting to communicate with a home accessory. The chime gave another laugh to point out just how stupid the entire situation had become.

I nibbled on my bagel. I was going to have to face up to a few things. Either:

1. I had been visited by the ghost of my dead stepsister.

2. I was going (or already was) crazy.

3. All the upheaval and changes of the past couple of months had caught up with me, resulting in a bad dream and delusions of paranormal activity. However, now that I'd gotten it all out of my system, everything would be fine. Nothing more than a nightmare brought on by change rather than too much dessert.

Anita believed in the other side. She thought most horror movies were basically documentaries, but I had always been more of a skeptic. As far as I could tell, dead was dead. Even if I made the assumption that there were ghosts, and that my stepsister had become one, why would Evelyn pick me to haunt? Why not haunt her dad or brother?

As for going crazy, although half of my genetic makeup had a leaning in that area, I refused to believe that I'd gone from sane to full-blown delusional in one night. After some consideration, I determined I didn't have any other crazy thoughts. I didn't think I was Napoleon, or that my bagel was an alien, and I didn't have voices in my head warning me about terrorist plots. Near as I could tell, I was still on the right side of sane. Granted, crazy people don't always know they're crazy, but it seemed to me if I could think through the issue so carefully, then I couldn't be insane. I took a deep breath and was almost 100 percent convinced.

I finished my bagel and brushed my hands off. I decided that, given my options, C was my best bet. The past few weeks had been brutal, with tons of changes and upheavals: my mom announcing she was getting married, meeting Dick, coping with Nathaniel's obvious disdain, having to move. It was no wonder I was seeing things. Come to think of it, it was surprising I hadn't been plagued with visions of ghosts or dancing hippos before now. That was practically proof of how sturdy my mental status was. I nodded stiffly at the wind chime and pulled the door closed on both the sunroom and any further thought of ghosts.

Chapter 7

I walked back through the living room and paused in the foyer. I placed my hand on the knob of the door that led to the west wing. It was ice cold. At first I thought it was locked, but the handle turned easily; the door itself was just stuck. When I pushed it, the door opened. I stepped inside.

The power was off in this wing, and although it was only the beginning of September, it felt like December. I sniffed. It smelled like mildew and a bit like the time my mom found a mouse dead in the walls of our last apartment. Dick might think the place only needed minor repairs, but it looked to me like this side of the house was in serious need of some major intervention. The hallway was wide, with paintings covered with sheets spaced every few feet along the wall. This must be the gallery. It certainly looked like I'd wandered down a random hallway of the Louvre.

I thought Dick was joking about there being a ballroom, but apparently not. The next room was huge and had a bank of windows along one wall. The curtains were a robin's egg–blue velvet, although there were dark splotches of what could be mold along the bottom of the fabric. I looked up. The ceiling had been painted white at one point but currently was sporting a serious case of yellow water spots like acne. At the far end of the room, next to a piano, was a riser, which must have been a platform for a live band. In the corner of the room there were a few pieces of furniture draped with dusty sheets.

I slid across the floor and jumped onto the stage. I looked over the empty room. It was irresistible. I broke out into song and added some killer dance moves.

When I finished the song, I flung my arms up before giving a bow. "Thank you, Seattle!"

I danced back across the floor, topping it off with a long slide into the gallery. That's when I heard clapping.

Oh shit.

Across the hall, a door was open. I took a few steps forward and peeked in. Unlike the rest of the wing, this room looked lived in. This had to be the library. The room was two stories tall and had floor-to-ceiling bookcases complete with a ladder that rolled around on a rail hung on the wall. There were a few leather club chairs scattered around. From where Nathaniel was sitting he could see out the door and across the hall, into the ballroom. He clapped slowly. My face flushed and suddenly the room didn't seem cold anymore. It felt like my ears were going to burst into flames.

"It's rude to spy on people. Why didn't you say anything?" My voice came out screechy.

"You wouldn't have heard me over your singing. I have to say, what you lack in talent you make up for with enthusiasm." He smiled.

"I didn't think anyone was home." The words squeezed out between my clenched teeth.

"I figured." He looked at my face and then stood up. "Don't be mad. I'm not making fun of you."

"Really?" I crossed my arms over my chest and cocked my head so that he could pick up on the sarcasm in my voice. I might not be able to sing, but I could smell mockery a mile away.

"Okay, fair enough. You're embarrassed and I made it worse. Do you want me to do something embarrassing to even the score? You want me to sing?"

Was he serious? The idea of him singing to me *was* surprisingly enticing. Unless he was up to something sneaky to make me feel even more humiliated. "Is this where you sing in an effort to make me feel better, but it turns out that you actually sing really well, so instead of feeling better, I actually feel worse?" I guessed.

He must have heard the skepticism in my voice, because he gave me a half smile. "I promise I'm a bad singer."

"Horrid or merely bad?"

He seemed to think it over. "I'm not sure. I've never sung for anyone else before."

That surprised me a little. "No church choir?"

"We were never a big churchgoing family."

"And you're willing to sing for me just to even the score?" Nathaniel was getting more intriguing by the minute.

"I feel like we've gotten off on the wrong foot." He looked down at his shoes. "Part of that might have been my fault."

"Might have been?" That was an understatement. He'd given me the impression he preferred we stay out of each other's way as much as possible until I left for college.

"Completely my fault." His eyes met mine, and I swallowed hard, aware suddenly of how blue his eyes were. I think I would have forgiven him for anything in that moment. Almost as if he'd read my mind, he broke the tension with a smile. "In fact, it's probably also my fault there's global warming and a shortage of honeybees. I apologize for that too."

I smiled back. "Don't think I'm letting you off for the global-warming thing, but for what it's worth, I hate bees." I walked past him and sat in his chair. It was still warm. He tossed me a worn quilt that had been on the floor and then sat down across from me. I picked up the book he had been reading, "The Tell-Tale Heart" by Poe. "You hang out in abandoned parts of houses just waiting for people to make idiots of themselves?"

"That was just luck. I would hang out here regardless. It's my favorite place."

I couldn't blame him. The room was huge but somehow felt cozy at the same time. In addition to the collection of worn, scarred leather chairs, there was a worn forest-green velvet chaise longue that sat under the big window at the end of the room. There was a stacked fieldstone fireplace that looked large enough to crawl around inside. There were candles on almost every flat surface, and I imagined how pretty they'd look at night. All in all, it was the kind of room I could enjoy hanging out in.

"It sucks this part of the house is shut off," I said.

"I sort of like it. Keeps it more private."

"And cold."

"And cold," he agreed. "I'll start a fire." Nathaniel stood and started to stack some wood in the fireplace. Either he had spent some time in the Boy Scouts or he had some specialized fire-building training. In no time flat he had the logs stacked expertly, with tightly twisted sheets of newspaper beneath them. God, he was good looking *and* handy. A thought occurred to me.

"I bet you're, like, king of the senior class here, huh?" I asked.

Nathaniel looked surprised. "Me?" He laughed. "Hardly. It's sort of hard to fit in unless you've been here forever."

"But you were born here, right? Your family, like, founded the island. Just how far back do people have to go before they decide you fit in?"

He lit a match and touched it to the newspaper under the logs. Once the paper caught fire, he blew on the small flame until it started to grow. "I didn't go to school here until last year.

My parents sent me to boarding school out in Massachusetts."

"Get out!" I tried to picture it. "Did you have to wear short pants with a blazer and tie?" I scootched to the end of my seat while I waited for his answer.

"We didn't wear short pants." He looked over his shoulder at me. "We did have ties, though, and the blazers with the fancy crest on the lapel."

"Let me guess, your dad went to the same boarding school?"

"And my grandfather, too."

I nodded. I could imagine Dick wandering around the grounds of a school full of picture-perfect brick buildings and trees where the leaves fell in color-coordinated piles.

"So why did you transfer here?"

"My mom was never a big fan of boarding school. I think she was behind the decision to have me move back." He brushed wood fibers from his pants. "Plus, stuff was getting hard for her with my sister, and I think she wanted the help." He sighed. "It was difficult as Evie got older. She had a hard time communicating. It made her frustrated. She'd throw tantrums."

"My mom mentioned that she had a disability."

"The doctor screwed up when Evie was born. The cord was wrapped around her neck and she was deprived of oxygen," he explained, still crouched beside the fireplace. "The doctor had been on the golf course drinking before he went to the hospital to deliver my sister. He didn't notice some of the readings on the monitor, so she was without oxygen long enough to cause brain damage. My parents sued him and won, but no amount of money was going to make her the way she would have been."

"That sucks," I said, stating the obvious.

"She had all sorts of problems with impulse control and communication. No matter how old she got, she was still like a two-year-old. She'd start crying or pick her nose in public. She'd wander off if you weren't paying attention. She could talk, but it wasn't always easy to figure out what she was saying."

Even though I was curious to hear more, I didn't want to pry. "That must have been hard," I said simply.

"Yeah. My mom was great with Evie, but my dad didn't have the patience. He'd get mad that she wasn't doing what he thought she should do and then mad at himself for being annoyed. Evie would pick up on those feelings and it would ramp her up further." Apparently satisfied with the fire, Nathaniel stood and brushed his hands off. "Anyway, I ended up moving back home."

"So much for my plan of riding your coattails to the heights of popularity, huh?" I asked.

He lost his serious look and managed a smile. "If you want to be popular, believe me, you'd be better off pretending you don't know me."

The room was warming up as the fire grew larger, and we sat quietly for a few minutes, enjoying the popping sounds and the flickering glow.

"You know, I think you're forgetting something if you want me to feel at home," I said.

Nathaniel started and then looked around. He gestured at a bag of cookies on the side table next to him. "Oh, sorry, you want some?"

"No, as I remember, you promised to sing for me."

He looked dubious. "Are you serious?"

"Deadly." I inwardly winced at my word choice, but pressed on. "You saw my humiliation and you offered—in fact, as I remember it, it may have been a promise—to even the score."

"I made you a fire." Nathaniel motioned to the fireplace with a flourish.

"Nice fire." I smirked. "Start singing, boarding-school boy."

"I don't know any songs," he protested, trying to weasel out of it with a pleading puppy dog pout. I pointed to the center of the room, and he must have realized that I wasn't the kind to give up easily. Resigned, he stood up and cleared his throat. If I wasn't mistaken, he was blushing a bit. "All right, but remember, you asked for it."

"Less warnings, more singing." I flopped back in my seat and waited. "Pick a song from your heart."

He stood in the center of the room and thought for a moment, and then belted out, "*Rudolph the red-nosed reindeer, had a very shiny nose.*"

I broke into giggles. He was right, he was closer to horrible than to merely bad. His voice warbled and sort of broke here and there. It was like a bad talent-show audition. At least he was giving it his all. As he got to the end of the song, he went down on one knee to really bring it home.

"Rudolph the red-nosed reindeer, you'll go down in hisssstooooorrrry!"

I gave him a standing ovation.

"Nicely done. I could tell you were one with the song." I linked my hands to show the connection.

"I think that's because I get the whole emotion of being left out of reindeer games."

"Ah, but don't forget the important part. In the end Rudolph is the hero. He's the one who lights the way for everyone."

Nathaniel snorted. "I'm not sure I'm much of the hero type, but that counts, right? We're starting over. Even?"

"Even." We reached to shake hands, and as soon as we touched, it felt like a current ran between the two of us. My heart sped up. Our eyes met. Nathaniel cleared his throat, and I realized he was trying to take his hand back and I was holding on to it with a death grip. I dropped his hand like it was a burning log. Oh God, I was turning into a stepbrother groper. He was nice to me, and the next thing he knew, I was hanging off him like a parasite. He was most likely grateful I hadn't thrown myself at his face for a tongue kiss.

I looked around desperately for something to change the subject. Then I saw it, a giant brass telescope facing out the window. "A telescope! I love these things," I yelled out. I ran over to it and peered through the eyepiece, gasping in surprise as the ocean jumped into perfect view. There was a ferry coming around the island and I could pick out individual people standing on the deck. "Wow. This is like being a pirate. I feel like Captain Hook."

"You should keep an eye out for humpback whales. They travel through here this time of year on their way from Alaska. Sometimes you can see them."

"Really? That's pretty cool. Sort of rude to spy on them, though, don't you think?" I raised an eyebrow. "Admit it, do you have a thing for whales?"

"I guess I never worried about being a whale stalker before. I promise to leave them unmolested from now on. But not the honeybees." Nathaniel flopped back down in his chair and flipped his book open. "Feel free to grab a book and cookie."

I saw a copy of the novel *Vanity Fair* on a shelf and pulled it out. Nathaniel passed me the cookie bag and I picked out a few. He draped his legs over the arm of the chair and started reading. I did the same, trying to look casual, but I couldn't forget how it had felt to touch his hand.

I peeked up from *Vanity Fair*. There was no doubt about it. I was falling for my stepbrother. Long term this would likely result in my ending up on a tacky daytime talk show with other people who had an unnatural love for their relatives, but for now, it felt good. We sat eating cookies and reading for the whole afternoon. Having someone you can talk to is cool, but it's been my experience that it is a lot harder to find someone you can be quiet with. Maybe this year wouldn't be so bad after all.

Chapter 8

I had assumed it would be hard to start at a new school for my senior year. However, I had completely underestimated just how craptastic it really would be.

Within twenty minutes of walking through the door, it was clear to me that everyone there had known each other since birth. Most likely their great-grandparents had gone to school together a zillion years ago, shortly after having enjoyed their trip on the *Mayflower*. I had the feeling that the terms "new kid" and "welcome wagon" weren't used very often around here.

When I walked into my first class, everyone turned around to stare at me and then began whispering to each other like crazy. Then they turned back around and looked at me again as if they were waiting for me to display some type of deformity or outrageous behavior. I went to the bathroom twice to make sure

I hadn't accidently written on my face with my ballpoint pen. I felt like a transfer student from Leper High with an uncontrolled case of Ebola. I had to fight the urge to run down the hallway yelling "BOOLA BOOLA BOOLA!!!" and waving my hands madly above my head just to give them a reason for all the strange looks.

I called Anita on my cell as I walked to lunch.

"It's worse than I imagined," I said before she even said hi.

"It's just first-day jitters."

"I'm not jittery. I'm miserable."

"You were always my glass-half-full kind of girl," Anita said. "A ray of sunshine."

"Easy for you to say, you're not here. You wouldn't believe some of these people. In my calculus class there's this guy . . ." I started to say before I realized that Anita was talking to someone else in the background.

"Sorry, what did you say?" she asked, tuning back in to me.

"I was telling you about this guy—"

"Cut it out!" Anita yelled, but she was giggling. Someone else was laughing in the background. "Sharon is being an idiot," Anita explained to me.

"Oh." I wasn't sure what to say. Sharon was in our class. She was one of those people who defined the term "class clown." She'd do anything for a joke. If she'd lived in medieval times, she would have been a full-time jester with bells hanging off her hat and giant pointy shoes curling up to her knees. Anita used to find her really annoying, but apparently not anymore. "Sounds like you guys are having a good time," I mumbled.

"It's totally not the same without you," Anita insisted. I could hear people laughing and a burst of conversation swirling around her. While it might not be the same, it didn't sound like it was that bad, either. "I should let you go. Go make some friends. Call me later, okay?" Anita clicked her phone off before I could tell her anything else.

I followed the herd of students to the cafeteria and shoved my phone back into my bag. I didn't know why I bothered to bring it. It wasn't like anyone wanted to talk to me.

My mom had offered to pack a lunch for me, but instead I had taken some money and planned to buy something. That was a mistake. At my old school we had a huge buffet that always had at least three options, all of them edible. We also had a salad bar. But Nairne's hot lunch program was a joke. Prison systems in flea-bitten third-world countries have better food programs. I'm not actually sure what gruel is, but I'm pretty sure that was what they were serving today.

When I got to the front of the line, I asked the lunch lady what it was and she said, "Hot lunch." Apparently, that was as descriptive as it was going to get. It was hot and it was designed to be eaten at lunch. Other than that there were no words to describe it. There wasn't even a candy/chip vending machine in the place, because some hippie contingent on the island had protested against it for being too corporate.

I looked around the cafeteria, but no one met my eye. I noticed nearly everyone had brought a lunch from home. I held my tray and waited to see if anyone was going to take pity on me, but it didn't look like it. The place wasn't that large, which meant I was going to have to ask to join someone else's table, take my gruel out into the hallway and eat it there, or skip lunch altogether. Then I saw Nathaniel sitting alone at a small round table by the window. I wove my way through the other tables and plopped my tray down. Nathaniel looked up at me.

"Mind if I join you?"

He paused, and for a split second I thought he was going to tell me that I couldn't. My throat started to tighten up, but then he pulled his tray back to make more room.

"Yeah, sure." He looked back down at his lunch bag and didn't say anything. I waited for him to ask how my first day was going, or if I liked my classes, or even to make some lame comment about the weather, but he just sat there contemplating his pile of chips.

As soon as I sat down I could hear a low-grade hum from the rest of the cafeteria. I turned around and everyone was looking at us. Some eighth grader one table over was sitting there with his mouth wide open while he stared at me. He was caught mid-chew and I could make out from where I was sitting that he was having bologna with that bright neon-yellow mustard.

"Problem?" I asked the kid, and he swallowed and looked away. I turned back around and poked my lunch. I wouldn't have been surprised if it started to fight back. "Good day so far?" I asked, trying to demonstrate how social skills work in polite society.

"Okay." Nathaniel shrugged.

So much for our big relationship breakthrough yesterday. He flipped through the book on the table, US history. He was either really into studying, fascinated by the Civil War, or ignoring me on purpose. I gave lunch another poke. In theory, emotional upset is supposed to make a person lose their appetite, but I was still starving.

This was stupid. I was going to dump the gruel, consider today a diet, and call Anita back. As long as I was going to be hungry, I didn't need to be starved of human interaction as well. I would force Anita to tell me what tasty thing they were serving at my old school. If she didn't feel like talking to me, at least she could hold up her phone and I could listen in on their discussion.

"Well, this has been fun, but I think I'm going to shove off." My chair let out a shriek as I pushed away from the table and started to stand.

Nathaniel looked up in surprise. "Wait a second." He glanced around and then gave a tired sigh. He spotted my tray. "Do you want half of my sandwich?" He held it out, and I had the sense he was offering more than turkey on whole wheat.

"That would be nice." I took the sandwich from him and sat back down. It wasn't much, but it was progress. "You can have some of mine if you want." I pushed my tray in his general direction. He pushed it right back.

"No matter what you might hear, I'm many things, but not crazy."

I laughed. I thought he was joking. He didn't even crack a smile.

Chapter 9

High schools are pretty much the same no matter where you go. There is an elite crowd, the losers, and the majority middle who are trying to either obtain elite status, avoid falling into the loser category, or are just doing their best to survive until graduation, when there's hope of a better life. There might be slight variations on what it takes to be in the cool crowd, but a safe bet is money, good looks, or athletic ability. If you manage to have two out of the three, or all three (a genetic home run), then you are destined to be popular.

I have zero out of the three. Generally, this doesn't bother me. I've never been one of those girls who read all the teen magazines trying to glean advice on how to be popular. I've never cut my hair like a pop star's. I never saw shaking my ass and a pair of pom-poms as a major life goal. Despite what the made-for-TV movies would lead you to believe is the dream of all teen girls, I have no major aspirations of having the star football player take me to prom, where I could lose my virginity in a glow of pink taffeta and the stink of a carnation corsage.

To be totally honest, most of the popular kids at my old school were dull. How many conversations can you have about the benefits of one brand of hairspray over another? I would rather tweeze my own eyebrows with kitchen tongs than spend hours dissecting who wore what to the dance and how so-and-so asked someone else's boyfriend to dance, and *oh my God* did you see her hair? I mean, really, who cares?

Anita and I weren't bitter outsiders who hated popular kids and secretly plotted their demise because in our hearts we wanted to be one of them. We had our own thing going. We had our own hangouts, friends, and hobbies. The popular crowd was an abstract concept for me. Sort of like the country Bora Bora. I know it exists, but it has no impact on my life whatsoever. I didn't expect things to be any different in my new school. Especially after all the strange looks I got by sitting with Nathaniel at lunch.

This is why I was totally shocked when Nicole Percy sat next to me on the bleachers in gym while our teacher set up the volleyball net. I hadn't been at this school for even a full day and I had already identified Nicole as the queen bee. I would have had to have severe social retardation not to notice that she was the most popular girl this island had going. She was most likely awarded prom queen status while still in elementary school. Nicole is one of those people who exude popularity. When she walks down the hall, people part in front of her and a gaggle of wannabes trail in her wake. She's blond (of course), and pretty, and her teeth are unnaturally white. Crest should sponsor this girl. When she sat next to me and smiled, I had to look away to avoid being blinded.

"So what do you think of Nairne?" Nicole tossed her hair, showing off shimmering highlights. "It must seem like the middle of nowhere after living in Seattle."

"It's okay." I wasn't stupid enough to insult her hometown. This was clearly one of those situations where if I called this place the armpit of Washington, the quote would end up in the local paper and I'd be pelted with rocks whenever I went out in public.

"It must be hard to transfer your senior year."

"You do what you gotta do." I was proud of myself for not calling her Captain Obvious. I couldn't figure out why she was talking to me. Either she mistakenly believed I was some sort of a volleyball genius and wanted me on her team, or she was working on her Girl Scouts Friendly to Strangers badge.

"If you need anything, you can just ask me," Nicole offered. Her eyes suddenly widened. "Hey, you should have lunch with me tomorrow. Then I can introduce you to everyone."

"Sure. That would be nice." I was careful to hide my surprise. Maybe the popularity threshold was lower here, and I was getting bonus points for being from the big city. Nicole was a bit perkier than I preferred, but who was I to be so choosy in the friend department? She seemed nice. It would be great to have someone to hang with, since it wasn't like I could call Anita every second, especially since she was so busy hanging out with Sharon.

Nicole smiled even wider. Her teeth looked like Tic Tacs. Perfectly white, perfectly shaped. "Do you want a ride home after school? I've got a car."

"I'd love a ride, but I live way out of town."

"I know where you live." Her eyes flashed. "Small town, you know, we know everything."

Chapter 10

I had pictured Nicole driving something that went with her personality. Maybe a car painted pink with Hello Kitty decals on it. I was surprised when she pulled up to the school door in an olive-colored Jeep with rust holes. The top was down and the sides were splattered with mud.

"Jump in." Nicole cranked the volume up on the radio.

I threw my backpack onto the floor and buckled in. Nicole was already peeling out. She gave a wave over her shoulder at a group of girls waiting for the bus. One of them was scowling at me. Uh-oh. The world order had been upset.

"I hope giving me a ride didn't put anyone out?"

"It's okay. I usually give Brit a ride, but she lives on the other side of the island altogether. She didn't mind taking the bus."

I hadn't met Brit yet, but I had the sneaking suspicion she

did mind taking the bus. She minded a lot. Great. One thing I didn't need at my new school was an enemy.

Nicole sped around a corner, and I grabbed on to the door handle for dear life. My hair was whipping around in the wind, and I suspected by the time I got back to the house it was going to look as if I'd styled it with a blender. Nicole's hair seemed to blow straight back. If anything, she was going to look better at the end of the ride.

"So you've lived here your whole life, huh?" I yelled over the radio.

"Born-and-bred native. I know it's dorky, but I love it. I like visiting the city, but I can't imagine wanting to live anyplace else." She looked over at me. "What about you? Are you dying to get off island?"

"Not dying exactly, but I miss the city. My friends and stuff."

"Not to mention how weird it must be to be living at Morrigan."

"Weird?"

"You know about the house and everything, don't you?"

"Of course," I said, bluffing. It's my experience that if you really want to know stuff, you are better off acting like you already have all the information. I stared out the window and didn't say anything else in hopes she would fill in the blanks.

"Does it freak you out at all?"

I shrugged.

"I hope you're not ticked that I asked. It's not like I believe that stuff. People around here just like to run their mouths. They're jealous. Besides, if there was any proof that it was murder, then Nathaniel or his dad would have been arrested."

Murder?! Holy shit. Did my mom know people on the island thought her new husband did in his first wife and daughter? I made a noncommittal noise.

"I don't think it would be a big deal at all except for the other stuff."

There was other stuff? Murder seemed like more than enough to me.

"What with the original Mrs. Wickham being kept locked in the attic way back when. And those kids that went missing? People figure there's too much smoke not to have any fire." Nicole swung into our long driveway with a spray of gravel. "Then there's *another* fatal accident in the family, so of course people assume there must be some kind of foul play, but it's not like things are connected, you know?"

I could feel myself starting to sweat. People locked in the attic? Missing kids? Had we moved into Hell House? "People love to talk," I murmured.

"Exactly." The gravel crunched under the car tires as we rounded the last bend. Nicole stopped the car. She pulled her hair back and looked up at the house. "I will admit if there was going to be a house on the island that's haunted, this would definitely be it. If a building could hold on to negative energy, this place would have more than its fair share. Not that I buy into what everyone says."

"People think the house is haunted," I said in a flat voice. I could feel the memory of the girl I saw by the window pushing to the front of my mind, and it took all the energy I had to shove it back down. I didn't want to go there. You start thinking there are ghosts, then voices speaking to you, and before you know it, you're bouncing around a rubber room wearing a tinfoil hat.

"Do you believe in ghosts?" Nicole asked.

"No." I hoped my voice sounded more confident than I felt. I looked over at Nicole. She was still staring up at the house. "Do you?"

She turned to look at me, and I leaned back quickly. Her eyes looked hungry and her teeth seemed not just shiny but also sharp. "Of course I believe," she said, her voice low.

"I should go." My hand fumbled for the door handle. I felt my chest release when it clicked open, and I spilled outside the Jeep. Every muscle in my body was screaming to run.

"We're still on for lunch tomorrow?" Nicole asked.

I looked back at her. She'd reverted to looking like your typical blond cheerleader. Her face was flushed from the wind, and I noticed for the first time that she had a sprinkle of light freckles across her nose and cheeks. Whatever I had seen a moment ago must have been just a trick of the light. Or of the mind. I took a deep breath. I just had a wee freak-out, which was understandable. There was all this new information, and the talk of ghosts on top of that was enough to give anyone a panic attack. It didn't mean there was anything wrong with me.

"Lunch tomorrow would be great," I said. I hefted my backpack and turned to go into the house. "Thanks for the ride."

"Keep your eyes open, Isobel," Nicole called out as she popped her Jeep in reverse to turn around. "Remember, ghosts don't care if you believe in them. They can still believe in you."

Chapter 11

"Mom!" I called out as soon as I opened the door. I stood in the doorway, my voice echoing in the marble foyer. I could hear the tall grandfather clock in the hall ticking, but that seemed to be the only sound. It felt like the house was holding its breath. Waiting for something.

Whoa. I had to stop thinking like that or I was going to freak myself out.

No one was home. There wasn't anything sinister about that. In fact, you could argue that having the place to myself was a good thing. I stood there a beat longer. I didn't want to shut the door behind me; I liked the idea of being able to escape easily. I forced myself to take a deep yoga breath.

I shut the door. No boogeyman lurched down the stairs. No ghosts floated out of the closet.

"I am not afraid," I said, reminding myself and also putting the house on notice just in case.

"Well, that's a good thing," a voice said.

I screamed and whirled around.

Nathaniel pushed open the swinging door from the kitchen. His mouth was stuffed with a bagel. He glanced around.

"What's wrong?" he asked.

"What's wrong? Are you trying to make me lose it? Why didn't you say something when I came in?"

"I didn't know I was supposed to. You called out for your mom. I didn't know I was required to announce my presence like it was role call." Nathaniel looked at me. His eyes softened and his voice lowered. "Are you okay?"

That was the million-dollar question, wasn't it? The fact that I had screamed like a four-year-old girl because someone told me a ghost story seemed to indicate that "okay" was not a term to use when describing me. That's when I noticed Nathaniel was holding a knife. A really sharp knife. My eyes locked onto the blade. I backed up a step until I was pressing against the front door.

"Well, that didn't take long," Nathaniel said.

I looked away from the knife and into his face. "What are you talking about?"

"So who told you?"

"No one told me anything," I said, trying to sound casual.

"Did they tell you I was a murderer, or in this version was it my dad? Obviously what happened couldn't have been an accident. I hope whoever it was took the time to mention the Wickham family curse."

"I don't know what you're talking about." My eyes flickered back to the knife.

"I was making a bagel." Nathaniel held out the knife, and I could see a smear of cream cheese on the blade.

"Oh." I wished the floor wasn't marble. All I wanted to do was dig a hole and crawl inside. Nathaniel was staring at me. His jaw was tight and I could see him swallow. It almost looked like he was trying not to cry. "You should feel free to ignore me. I'm a huge drama queen. Just ask my mom," I said.

"Whatever." Nathaniel kicked the swinging door to the kitchen open and walked out.

There went any progress we'd made in being friends. It was going to take more than shared lunches and singing Christmas carols to get over the fact that I'd basically implied he was capable of murdering his own family. I followed him into the kitchen. Nathaniel was putting clean dishes back into the cupboard.

"Look, I'm sorry," I said.

"You better be careful, I've got a ladle." Nathaniel waved a giant soup ladle back and forth. "You never know what a trained killer can do with an innocent-looking kitchen utensil."

"I don't think you're a trained killer."

"So should I be insulted that you think I'm an amateur killer?" He pulled another item out of the dishwasher. "Uh-oh. An ice cream scoop. You better back up before I decide to use it."

"Anyone ever tell you that you make it very difficult for a person to apologize?"

"No, I don't have any friends who would pass on that kind of information. Remember, I told you I don't get invited to play any reindeer games."

"You could have warned me, said something about what people thought. You had to know someone was going to say something."

Nathaniel banged a pot down on the counter. "Right. Hey, Isobel, welcome to the family. By the way, you should know most people at school think I killed my mom and sister. Turns out, when they died, I didn't think to have an alibi set up. Of course neither did my dad, and he has motivation, too, because he got the life insurance payout. Sure, it could have been an accident, but that doesn't give people much to talk about, does it? Don't let that bother you, though, just make yourself at home. Have a nice day at school." Nathaniel pulled another pan out of the dishwasher and practically tossed it into the cabinet. "For some reason, I'm guessing that wouldn't have been a great opener."

He had a point, but still. "You could have found another way to say it."

He turned his back to me and continued to put the dishes away. "Maybe I'm a lousy communicator, but I couldn't think of a great way to drop that kind of news." There was an unmistakable edge to his voice.

I leaned against the counter and watched him. "I guess not,"

I agreed, hoping I hadn't ruined everything by acting so jumpy. One thing I was sure of, I didn't want to lose the rapport we'd started building. "If it'll make you feel better, I could tell you something embarrassing about my family," I offered.

He paused, as if weighing his response carefully. "You aren't going to sing again or anything, are you? I've already had enough trauma in my life." This time, his tone was light.

I swatted him with one of the kitchen towels. "I'm being serious. I'm trying to even the score."

"Okay." Nathaniel jumped up so he was sitting on the wooden butcher-block counter. "Spill it."

Suddenly I felt nauseated. What had I been thinking when I'd opened my mouth? I only had one really big family secret, but other than Anita, I'd never told anyone about my dad. It would have been easier to tell someone that my dad had leprosy or was a terrorist than that he had a mental illness. It was just a small step from someone knowing about my dad's condition to their wondering just how much like my dad I might be. I didn't need anyone, Nathaniel especially, thinking I was crazy.

"Forget it."

"Forget it? You promised me a story of humiliation. What happened to evening the score?"

"I decided I don't want to." I grabbed my backpack and went to turn around. Nathaniel jumped down and grabbed my elbow.

"Hang on." He stepped in front of me to block my path. "You can't just decide not to."

"Of course I can. Look at that, I just did." I tried to keep my voice casual, but my heart was beating hard and fast. I tried to step around him, but instead of letting me pass, he lowered his head to stare into my eyes.

"What's the matter, are you afraid?"

I refused to look away or blink, lest he take it as a sign of weakness and pounce. "Maybe I don't feel like telling you my secrets. It's not like you told me yours. Nicole did."

"Don't be pissed at me. You brought the whole thing up."

"And now I'm dropping it."

"You're afraid," he said, crossing his arms.

"No, I'm not."

"Yes, you are. You can say what you want; I know I didn't kill anyone. I've got nothing to be ashamed of. Clearly, *you've* got some issues, though."

"I'm not ashamed of anything."

Nathaniel raised one eyebrow. "Sure."

"I'm not." I pressed my lips together. This is why I never missed having siblings. I'd had a stepbrother for less than a week and we were already fighting. It was just a matter of time until someone told us to take a time-out and we'd have to sit in different corners. "I don't have to tell you anything." I meant to say it firmly, but it came out more like a scared whisper.

Nathaniel looked at me for a moment more and then shrugged. "Got me there. Well, this heart-to-heart has been fun. If you'll excuse me, I've got homework." He turned and left the kitchen, leaving me trying to catch my breath. I could hear him as he raced up the stairs. My legs suddenly felt weak, and I leaned against the doorframe. I could feel the notches in the wood where generations of Wickham kids had marked their heights.

I didn't even have to look to know I didn't measure up.

Chapter 12

I had to wonder how Morrigan could have a ballroom but no wireless internet. Where were the priorities? The only internet connection was the computer in Dick's study. Apart from the fact that I wasn't keen on spending any time in a room stuffed with dead animal heads, there was the very real chance that Dick would discover that I'd been digging through his family dirt. I was willing to bet his "ho ho ho, we're all one big, happy family" act would be over. If I was going to play Nancy Drew, then I needed to be clever. Since Nathaniel wasn't talking to me, I couldn't ask him for a ride to the library, and Nicole already knew too much, so involving her wasn't an option. It was times like this I could see the value of having a driver's license.

When we lived in the city, being able to drive seemed like more of a hassle than it was worth. Traffic was lousy and there was never anyplace to park once you got there. There was usually someone around who could drive me, and if there wasn't, then I could always take public transportation. On Nairne Island there was no public transportation. Not even some sort of hippie VW bus that ran on old cooking oil. The school bus only ran twice a day, so it was less than perfect for my purposes. This is why I was in the garage trying to clean what looked like a century's worth of cobwebs off a bike.

My mom poked her head in the garage. "Are you sure you don't want me to give you a ride?"

"No, thanks. I want to have my own mode of transport, instead of having to wait on other people." Something fell off the back of the bike and skittered away. I yanked the bike out. The tires looked a bit squishy, but most likely they would make it into town once I pumped them up. There was a rusted basket fixed to the handlebars, and I dumped my backpack in there. "Besides, biking will be fun."

My mom didn't look so sure. She didn't say anything, but I could tell she was thinking I'm not really the cycling sort. To be fair, it's not just cycling—the term "sporty" isn't used to describe me. I don't run unless something is chasing me, and I have some kind of visual-spatial ball deficiency. I'm always that person in gym class who gets smacked in the face with the ball. Volleyball, softball, basketball, those nasty, stinging red rubber dodgeballs . . . you name it and I've eaten it.

It only took a few minutes to pump the tires up, but I was

already a little winded from the effort by the time I led the bike out into the yard and straddled it. The bike was pale blue and looked like it was from the 1950s. I told myself the vintage look was in and began pedaling. I would have sworn the road into town had been flat yesterday, but now that I was biking, it was clear there were hills. Lots of hills. It was also clear that my cardio levels were that of an eighty-year-old woman who smoked a few packs of unfiltered cigarettes a day. Nathaniel passed me in his car. He slowed down as he went by. I would have said something, but I was sucking air for all it was worth. He shook his head and then sped off. All I could do was hope that my trip to the library would be worth it.

The library on Nairne is in the center of downtown, the term "downtown" being used fairly liberally. The entire thing is only four blocks long, over half of which consist of stores that cater to the tourists and are only open during the summer months. If you want a T-shirt, cheap fudge, or homemade soap with seashells floating in it, then downtown Nairne is your shopping paradise. The library is in a converted house and shares the space with the post office.

The librarian (who also does double duty as the postmaster) watched me very carefully when I walked in, as if she thought I might suddenly start stuffing paperbacks under my shirt and make a run for it.

"Can I help you?" Her smile was so tight, I wondered if she'd been sucking on lemons. I could see from where I was standing that her lipstick had bled into all the creases around her mouth. It was like her lips had grown tentacles. She also needed to do her roots. She had a halo of gray all around her face.

"I'm fine, thanks." I glanced around the room.

"I'm afraid only residents can check out materials."

"I am a resident."

Her eyes widened and her lips pressed together even more tightly. "Ah." She shifted like she'd just noticed her shoes were too tight. "Well. I heard Mr. Wickham's new wife had a child. Welcome to the island."

"Thanks. Is there a computer I can use?"

"Of course. It's over in the corner. There's a teen section too, under the window. I'll get a card made up for you so you can check things out. Things can be borrowed for two weeks, with a maximum of ten items. There's a twenty-minute rule on the computer if someone else wants to use it. We also forbid anyone going to pornographic sites."

"Got it. Two weeks, ten things, twenty minutes, and no porn."

The librarian gave me another lemon-sucking smile. I could tell she was one of those people who hated teens and secretly believed we were all drug-taking hooligans. I smiled back and began to wander up and down the aisles between the shelves. The bell over the door rang again and a woman backed in with two large boxes that she carried over to the postal counter. I could hear the women whispering, and when I looked over, they were both staring at me.

I sat down at the computer and pulled up Google. There were a few travel articles on the island (apparently Melanie's Sea Shanty Bed-and-Breakfast had the best blueberry muffins on the West Coast) and some random articles on its history, but other than a short piece mentioning a funeral, I couldn't find anything on Dick's first wife and daughter. The story might have been too small to be picked up by the larger papers. I tried a few other searches. I found an article on West Coast architecture that mentioned Morrigan. Apparently the Wickhams used to offer house tours during the summer. In the summer of 1957, one of the tourists took a nasty fall down the stairs, and after that the house had been closed to the general public. The article didn't mention whether the tourist had recovered, but it would have said something if the tourist had died, wouldn't it?

"Ah. Morrigan," a voice said behind me. I jumped and spun around. Jesus. She must have been wearing super-quiet librarian shoes. It was another librarian, younger than the first. She had a nice smile and I noticed she was pretty, but she needed some major fashion advice. Her outfit was heavy on the pastels and had shoulder pads. Her name tag said *Mandy*. She looked over my shoulder at the screen, and I cringed.

"Uh." I couldn't tell if this was worse than being caught with porn.

She looked me in the eye. "Researching the island history for school?"

Was she really going to give me this easy out? "Um, yeah. I have a paper."

"You might want to check out the archives section. There are a couple amateur historians on the island. They've collected quite a bit of stuff. The local paper hasn't yet caught up to the idea of having an online presence." She motioned over to a shelf on the left. "You can't check things from the archive out, but you might find what you're looking for in there. There are old letters from people who used to live here and copies of the local paper."

"Thanks." I walked over to the shelf, where there were three file boxes. I hefted one onto the closest table and lifted the top off. The box was divided into sections and I grabbed a file at random. It was an old copy of the *Nairne News*. The headline read MISSING TEENS ASSUMED DEAD. I felt the hairs on the back of my neck prickle. The box was full of documents. All day long I had been looking forward to finding out more, but now that it was in front of me, I wasn't sure I wanted to know.

"It's good to see people your age interested in history," the librarian said. "You know what they say, don't you? Those who don't learn from history are doomed to repeat it."

After she left, I pulled the other two boxes onto the table. I started pulling out files, trying to figure out if there was a particular order to everything. There were clippings from the newspaper on various island events: Fourth of July parades, school plays, the election of a new police chief. The older clippings were yellow and brittle. Overall, Nairne Island wasn't shaping up to look like a very happening place. Then I saw something that caught my eye. It was from 1924 and the black headline was in giant forty-plus-size font.

The Island Loses One of Its Own in Tragic Accident

Molly O'Shannon, 17, was found dead early yesterday morning at the Morrigan estate, her place of employment. Jonathon Mark, the butler, found her body at the bottom of the front hall stair. Cause of death is a broken neck following a fall.

Miss O'Shannon had lived on the island for just over a year, working as a maid at the Morrigan estate. "Terrible loss. She was a lovely girl. We never had any problems with her," said Mr. Wickham, expressing his sorrow on behalf of the entire family. Reports are that the Wickhams have offered to pay the costs of the funeral for the girl. A service will be held at the Presbyterian Church this coming Saturday at 2 p.m. All are welcome.

I dug the first article I'd seen back out. A quick check of the date at the bottom showed that the paper was just over twenty years old.

Missing Teens Assumed Dead

The search for two missing sisters was called off today. Both girls, ages 18 and 16, have been missing since May 30.

The girls were last seen at a party on Tara Cove Beach on the night of the thirtieth. Three witnesses recall them stating that they were planning to go "ghost hunting" at the Morrigan estate. Witnesses have also confirmed the girls had been drinking. Early search efforts focused on the grounds of Morrigan and the surrounding area, but no sign of the girls was found.

"It's like they simply disappeared," Holly Watson, a school friend of the girls, said at a candlelit prayer vigil held last week. The girls' parents declined to comment for this story, although Mabel Brink, a family member, stated: "These were good girls. Whatever happened to them, they didn't deserve it. All those people who said they ran off should be ashamed of themselves."

Constable Edmunds stated that it wasn't viable to keep the search going after so much time with no iden-tified leads. "Our hope is that the girls caught a ride with someone to the mainland. It's possible that they're fine, but they're afraid to call home knowing they'll be in trouble. Worst-case scenario is they went off swimming or boating late at night and had some sort of accident. We've filed missing-person reports and at this point there isn't much else we can do."

Anyone with any news on the missing girls is encouraged to call Constable Edmunds.

I rubbed the back of my neck. It might have been all the small, blurry print or the dust, but I was getting a headache. I still needed to find something recent about Nathaniel's family. At the back of the next box I found it. There was a picture under the headline. I recognized Nathaniel's mom from the picture in his room.

Catastrophic Boating Accident Claims Two Lives

Marine investigators declared yesterday that Sylvia Wickham and her daughter, Evelyn Wickham, were both casualties of the February 9 boating accident.

The Wickhams' boat, *The Tempest*, was found floating off Porto Cove Bay early in the morning of February 10. There was no one aboard and no damage to the boat. No life jackets were found on the boat. Mr. Richard Wickham reported his wife and daughter missing on Thursday evening when they failed to return home from what was planned to be a short sail. Mrs. Wickham's body was recovered two days later, but Evelyn, age 10, has not been found. She is presumed dead at this time.

Investigators could determine no cause for the accident. Mrs. Wickham was an experienced sailor and there were no indications that the boat had any mechanical problems. The weather on the day Mrs. Wickham and her daughter disappeared was a sunny 38 degrees with light wind, which should have posed no difficulties. Although it is early in the season, it was not uncommon for Mrs. Wickham to take the boat out unattended. The police have stressed there were no signs of foul play and have declared the incident to be a tragic accident.

Mrs. Wickham and her daughter, Evelyn, are survived by Richard and Nathaniel Wickham. A private memorial service for family only is being held this weekend.

I put the paper down and rummaged through part of the box. It was clear that the Wickham family had had more than their share of trouble. Still, the boating accident sounded shifty to me. Why did the police feel it was so important to stress that there were no signs of foul play?

The librarian cleared her throat. That's when I noticed it had grown dark outside.

"We'll lock up soon," she said softly.

I looked down at my watch. Shit. I'd lost all sense of time. It was already almost seven. My mom must be freaking out. I grabbed my phone out of my bag. I'd turned the ringer off when I'd gotten to the library. Shit. Six missed calls.

"Thanks for telling me about the archives," I said, shoving the files back into the boxes.

"I hope you found what you were looking for." Mandy pulled on the sleeves of her cardigan. She was wearing about a hundred small silver bangles on her arm.

"Most of it."

She had a smudge of gray dust on her cheek. I had one more question she might be able to help me with, and after all, if you can't ask your librarian, who can you ask?

"Have you ever heard anything about a member of the Wickham family being kept locked in an attic?" I asked. I had to hand it to the librarian. She didn't look surprised or ask me how I could have become part of a family that I didn't know basic things about, like if they'd had relatives in the belfry.

"People at school telling you stories?"

"So it's just a story?" I felt a band of tension around my chest loosen up.

"Things weren't quite right with the first Mrs. Wickham. Let's see, she would have been your stepdad's great-great-grandmother, I think. Of course, it isn't clear what exactly the issue was, but she was mentally ill."

"So they locked her in an attic?" My voice sounded panicked to my ears.

"It was the 1800s. Mental illness was something deeply shameful at that time. The kind of thing you locked away, so it didn't contaminate everything else. I suspect the family thought they were doing the right thing, even if it must have been terrible for her."

The way she was looking at me made me wonder if she somehow knew about my dad. As soon as the thought came into my head, I knew it was paranoid. At this rate I'd soon start thinking that the government was tapping my phone and start wearing foil wrapped around my head to repel the gamma waves from Planet Nine. I felt my phone vibrate.

"I should get going." I started to grab my things and shove them into the bag. Suddenly I wanted—no, I needed—to get out of the library.

"Don't be a stranger!" The bangles on her wrist jingled as she waved good-bye.

I wove my way back through the stacks. The older librarian was standing near the door, her hands twisting back and forth. She looked startled when she saw me, scared almost.

"Is everything okay?" she asked.

I knew she was really asking about me, if I was okay. She could tell something was wrong. But I didn't feel like lying. "No," I replied as I slipped past her and into the night.

Chapter 13

My mom and I were never close. We never stayed up late into the night watching girly movies in our pj's and giving each other manicures. We never had heart-to-heart conversations where she shared her embarrassing childhood moments as a way to provide me with meaningful lessons on what I should do with my life. On the positive side, we also didn't hate each other. We didn't slam a lot of doors and have screaming matches that ended with someone yelling out "I hate you!" Neither of us ever slapped the other or threw anything. I knew she loved me, but I also knew, even without her saying anything, that she thought her life would have been easier without me. My mom and I were more like roommates. Generally we liked each other, but we preferred to keep our distance. My mom never said anything to confirm my suspicions, but I'm pretty sure I wasn't the daughter she had in mind. She would have preferred a bubbly cheerleader type, someone who would want to shop with her and swap beauty tips. We didn't like the same things. She didn't understand my worldview, and I didn't have a clue about how her mind worked either.

Take, for example, our current situation. I would assume that most people would want to know if they were living in a house that could be considered cursed, or at the very least, a house that met the minimum standards for unlucky. My mom didn't see things that way at all.

"Is this a joke?" She crossed her arms and glared at me from the living room doorway. I folded my legs underneath me on the sofa.

"Um. No." What sort of sense of humor did she think I have?

"I don't believe you, Isobel."

"Mom, this isn't the kind of thing I'd ever make up. The documents are in the library. They're a matter of public record. Seriously. You can look them up yourself."

"That's not what I meant. I meant I can't believe you would stoop this low."

"Low? Library research is low?"

"You better zip up that attitude right now."

I pressed my lips together to keep from saying anything. I love how when you have an opinion different from your parent's it's an "attitude."

"How much do you even know about these people?" I asked.

"These people? These people are your new family."

"This isn't my family! This is the guy you married and his kid. Call me picky, but I like to have a higher threshold on who I consider family. You married Dick after three months! How well can you know someone in three months?" I took a deep breath and let it out. "Look, all I'm trying to do is point out that there's a lot more going on in this house. I thought you'd *want* to know all this history."

"What is going on, Isobel? What is it that you're trying to say? That Richard did something unsavory? He told me all about the suspicions and gossip people were throwing around. Do you know how much that hurt him? That was his wife and child who died. This is a small town. When there isn't enough drama to gossip about, people make it up, and they don't care who it hurts."

"They don't have to make much up, Mom. Dick's wife and daughter are dead. That's not gossip, that's a fact. Then you add in all the other weird stuff about this house, and it's suspicious."

"Weird stuff about the house. So the ghost you think you saw makes you think it's haunted."

"I'm not saying I saw a ghost and I don't know if it's haunted. I'm just saying . . ." My voice trailed off.

"You realize how crazy that sounds, don't you?"

I sucked in a deep lungful of air. I couldn't believe she'd said that, and the hurt must have shown on my face, because she rolled her eyes.

"Oh, for crying out loud. It's an expression. If it stings, it's because it's true. It does sound crazy. I know you didn't want to move here, and believe me, you've made it very clear what you think of Richard. Either you're dragging all this stuff out to try to upset me or you're doing it on a subconscious level. I certainly hope this isn't on purpose, but either way, I want you to drop it."

"Fine. Consider it dropped, but don't say I didn't try warning you." I brushed past her and ran up the stairs. I yanked open the door to my room, and that's when I noticed it. I ran my hand across the doorjamb outside my room. There were four holes in the wood. I shut the door with a quiet click and took a closer look. There were two additional screw holes in the door that lined up with the other four on the frame. I let my fingers trail over the holes as if I could read them like braille. No doubt about it. There had been a lock on the door at one point. A lock on the outside, meant to keep someone in.

Chapter 14

The next morning passed uneventfully, but I still wasn't sure what to expect at lunchtime. I stood at the door to the cafeteria with my brown paper bag in hand. Say what you like about me, but at least I was smart enough to learn I should pack my own lunch. Scanning the sea of teenagers, I tried to spot Nicole among the tables. I wasn't sure if the invitation to sit with her at lunch was still on or if she had made the offer in haste as a result of volleyball-induced hysteria and now was going to pretend it never happened.

"Hey! Isobel! Over here." Nicole stood up so I could see her. She was waving madly like she was part of the ground crew of Chicago O'Hare airport. I could see a few people look over in surprise. I pulled my shoulders back and tried to exude the aura of someone who was used to being the center of attention. I wove through the tables. I paused when I passed Nathaniel's table. He glanced up from his book and then over at Nicole.

"Well, well. Look who's managed to upgrade herself to the inner reindeer circle her first week."

"You have a problem with that?"

"Nope. Just didn't picture you as the cheerleader type. Are they going to get you a set of black pom-poms?"

"Ha-ha. I'm not becoming a cheerleader."

"Never say never, Blitzen." He looked back down at his book. Clearly the conversation was over.

I walked away without saying anything else, mostly because I couldn't think of a really good comeback. Nicole pulled out a chair next to her to make room for me.

"What did Nathaniel say?"

"Uh, just telling me some stuff for our history class."

"He can join us too if he wants."

I peeked over at Nathaniel. I couldn't picture him surrounded by all this estrogen. Most of Nicole's friends were heavy on the girly girl look. There wasn't a single shade of pink not represented at the table. I pulled down my black T-shirt. "I'm not sure he would want to. He and I aren't really close friends or anything."

"He doesn't have any friends," the girl across the table said.

"Don't be such a snot. Nathaniel's her brother."

"Stepbrother," I clarified.

"See that, even his stepsister can tell he's a freak and doesn't want to be related to him." The girl looked at me. "I'm Brittany. Everyone calls me Brit." She pointed around the table. "This is Samantha, but we call her Sam, and Jenni, with an *i*, not a *y*."

"I'm Isobel, also with an *i*." No one laughed.

"Don't call him a freak. God, just because he isn't like everyone else," Nicole grumped, stabbing at her salad. I felt like I should be the one defending him.

"Isn't that the definition of 'freak'? They don't fit in?" Brit flipped the top of her sandwich off and began picking through the contents. She left the bread and ate some of the turkey lunch meat. She raised a hand to stop Nicole before she could speak. I could see a glob of mayonnaise on the side of one finger. "I'm joking."

"Don't you think it's hard enough for Isobel to be new without you slagging her family?"

"I'm fine," I said, but no one seemed to hear me.

"I didn't slag anyone. I made one flip comment. Maybe Isobel shouldn't be so high-strung that she can't take a joke."

"I can take a joke," I said, but again no one was listening to me.

"Maybe you should think about what you say before it comes out of your mouth."

"Don't worry about me. It's no big deal." I wondered if

I was only thinking I was saying anything out loud, because as far as I could tell from the reactions around me, I wasn't making a sound.

"Whatever." Brit's chair screeched as she pushed back from the table. Sam and Jenni both had their mouths open in perfect Os. Brit stomped out of the cafeteria. Nicole went back to harpooning her salad.

"I brought Cheetos. Anyone want one?" I offered, holding out my Ziploc baggie. It wasn't a great conversational opener, but it was all I had. Sam pulled back like I had held out a bag of steaming dog poop.

"Do you have any idea how much fat and salt are in those things?" Sam's nose wrinkled up.

I pulled out a Cheeto and looked it over. I wondered if she thought I didn't know that it was constructed completely of fat and salt. That's what made it taste so good. I popped it in my mouth and rubbed the orange cheese powder off on my pants.

"You're going to have to watch what you eat," Nicole said. "It might seem like a small thing, but the wrong food can really slow you down."

"Slow me down? Where am I going?"

"Cheerleading. We're all on the squad. I talked to Ms. Lancaster, and she says you can be an alternate." Nicole smiled like she was announcing I had won the lottery.

"Me?"

"Don't worry about the alternate thing, it's just a formality. You'll have a uniform and everything, and there's no reason you can't cheer at most of the games. Ms. Lancaster can't make you officially on the squad because you weren't here for tryouts."

"I can't be a cheerleader."

"Of course you can. We've already fixed it all up. Our whole group is on the squad. You're going to love it."

"I've never cheered in my life." I looked around in confusion. I could see Nathaniel watching what was happening with a smirk on his face. "I'm not even sure I can do a cartwheel."

"Tell you what, I'll give you a ride home today and I'll show you some of the routines. You'll pick them up in no time. I'm a great teacher."

Nicole, Jenni, and Sam were all smiling at me as if they expected me to break into tears of joy like a newly crowned Miss America. I could tell they thought they had done me some sort of huge favor. How do you tell someone who thinks cheerleading is some sort of divine gift that you think it's stupid? Spelling things out in front of large crowds while wearing a short skirt was not remotely my idea of a good time. But I didn't want to offend the only girls who seemed interested in being my friends. If I insulted them, I had a feeling I'd be even less likely to befriend anyone else.

I thought quickly. "You know, I'd love to, because I'm

sure it's super fun and all, but I'd hate for people to be upset that I snuck onto the squad." I gave a shrug like I was full of remorse and wanted nothing more than to prance about on the sidelines of various sporting events.

"Don't worry about it," Nicole assured me. "I'll take care of everything. You're one of us now. No one bothers our group."

"I guess I owe you," I said slowly, giving her what I hoped looked like a sincere smile.

"I guess you do," Nicole said with a wink.

Chapter 15

"You have to give me a tour." Nicole stood in the foyer next to me, her eyes sparkling with anticipation.

"There's not much to see. Bedrooms, kitchen, living room. The usual." I could feel my face flush.

"Are you kidding me? Look at this place. It's like Buckingham Palace or something. My mom is going to freak out when she hears I've been in Morrigan. She's always wanted to see the inside of this place."

Suddenly I wondered if it was even okay that I'd invited her over. It hadn't occurred to me to check with Dick, but maybe he was weird about having visitors in his house. Knowing Dick, he would have potential guests fill out some sort of application form, sign a waiver, complete a confidentiality agreement, or possibly take a qualifying quiz before they were let in the front door. He'd probably also want them to demonstrate that their relatives came over on the *Mayflower*. After all, it wasn't inviting someone over to my house, it was inviting them to an *estate*.

Nicole sat down on the bottom step. "This must be exactly where the maid died in the twenties. She was found here in a puddle of blood with her eyes wide open." Nicole ran her hand over the stair. For some reason, her fascination made me uncomfortable. It wasn't anything different from what I felt when I walked up the stairs, but it seemed like the kind of thing you shouldn't comment on. I think Miss Manners must have some sort of rule about how early you can bring up references to fatal accidents that happened in someone else's home.

"They say she was having an affair with the Wickhams' son."

"What?" That tidbit hadn't made the local paper.

"That's why they killed her. She was pregnant and the Wickhams didn't want a lowly maid as the mother of their grandchildren. Apparently, the son was really in love with her. Real Romeo and Juliet stuff, a forbidden love."

"So you think someone pushed her down the stairs?"

"That's what everyone says. There was a fight where the parents tried to pay her off, but when she wouldn't take the money, Mrs. Wickham snapped and pushed her. She broke her neck when she fell. Then they got away with the whole thing. They called it an accident and no one dared to question them. The butler found her in the morning lying at the bottom of the stairs. They say the blood never came out of the floorboards."

I could feel my heart picking up speed, but I shook it off. "Well, you can report back, there isn't any blood and the floor is marble. Maybe they just didn't have Lysol with bleach back then."

Nicole laughed and stood up. "Okay, fair enough. Let's go in the backyard, where we can jump around."

"Look, about this cheerleading thing—"

"Hi, Nathaniel!" Nicole cut me off. She pushed her shoulders back and jutted one hip out. I looked up the stairs and watched him lope down. "Great place you've got here."

"You know what they say, no place like home."

Nicole burst into laughter as if he'd said the funniest thing ever known to man. She placed her hand on Nathaniel's forearm and leaned in. "You're wicked."

"That's the rumor about town," Nathaniel said, directing a meaningful look my way. Nicole gave another tinkling laugh. "What brings you to our humble abode?"

"What, your company isn't enough?"

If she kept laying it on so thick, I was going to gag. "Nicole gave me a ride home," I said, interjecting myself into all the flying hormones in the room.

"I'm teaching Isobel some of the cheerleading routines."

I felt like pounding my head on the wall. I didn't look at Nathaniel, because I knew if I did I'd want to smack the smirk right off his face.

"Cheerleading?" I heard the amusement in his voice.

"I haven't exactly agreed to join," I said.

"But you have to! All the popular girls are on the squad," Nicole insisted.

"Yeah, Isobel, all the popular girls are on the squad," Nathaniel echoed. I could see his lip twitching as he tried to hold in a laugh.

"Nathaniel, are you one of those cheerleader haters?" Nicole put on a frowny face and leaned forward for maximum cleavage exposure. Nathaniel looked. Of course he looked. She practically was shaking her breasts in his face. If he wasn't careful, a wayward nipple was going to take out one of his eyes. Okay, so it would have been impossible for him not to notice. However, he didn't have to keep noticing. It was like his eyes had homing beacons on her boobs.

"Who could hate you?" Nathaniel answered, finally pulling his gaze away from her chest. I fought the urge to choke on all the cheesy lines floating around. I guess this was one type of reindeer game he was comfortable playing.

Nicole shoved him lightly, one of those pushes that's really just an excuse to touch a guy's arm.

"Well, I guess we'd better start that practice, huh?" My voice came out louder than I expected. Both Nathaniel and Nicole looked over at me in surprise.

"I wouldn't want to stand in the way of school spirit," Nathaniel said. "You guys have fun."

"You can watch us if you want," Nicole invited in a purry voice.

"No, you can't." The last thing I needed was Nathaniel watching me attempt one of my deformed cartwheels. Nicole scowled like a pouty child who'd been told that playtime was over.

"I've got calculus anyway," Nathaniel said.

"Maybe next time?" Nicole asked.

"Wouldn't miss it." Nathaniel ambled off to the kitchen. Nicole and I watched him walk away.

"So what was that?" I asked when I was sure he couldn't hear us.

"What do you mean?"

I raised one eyebrow in response.

"What? He's cute. He might be your brother, but you must have noticed."

"He's my stepbrother."

"Same thing. You have to invite me to spend the night some time. He's one I'd love to catch half-asleep," Nicole said, licking her lips. An image of Nathaniel in his boxer shorts shot into my head. I forced it away on the off chance she could read minds.

"I'm not sure he's looking to date anyone," I cautioned.

Nichole suddenly looked concerned. "It doesn't bother you that I like him, does it?"

"What? No, of course not." But her suggestion made me blush.

"I mean, he's your brother. It's not like *you* could date him."

I fought the urge to point out, *again,* that he was only my stepbrother.

"Plus, he's not really your type," Nicole added.

"What do you mean?" I asked.

Nicole's eyes widened and her mouth made a tiny Life Savers O. I had a feeling I knew exactly what she meant. He was out of my league.

"Oh, you know—I picture you liking the typical bad boy. A tattooed guy who wears a leather jacket and plays in a band." Her hands waved around as if she was trying to distract me from what she was trying hard not to say, which was that I was too low rent for someone like Nathaniel. "Hey, before we practice, do you think you could show me the attic, where they locked up the crazy Mrs. Wickham way back when?"

I was getting a crystal-clear idea of why Nicole wanted to be my friend. It had less to do with her desire to be all Mother Teresa to the new kid and way more with seeing me as her all-access pass to Morrigan . . . and Nathaniel.

Chapter 16

I was on a boat. The varnish on the wooden deck was hot from the sun; I could feel the heat through the soles of my feet. The air rushed by, smelling of salt and freshly washed cotton, but it was cold. I looked up. There was a green-and-white-striped sail pushing the boat forward as we cut a line through the white-tipped waves. I could see seagulls racing alongside, swooping up and down. There was a picnic set up on the deck of the boat. Deviled eggs, turkey sandwiches, a bunch of green grapes, and a pan of brownies cut into perfect squares. There was a single brownie resting on a napkin with a half-moon bite taken out of it.

It should have been an ideal scene. They put images like this on postcards. But instead of feeling relaxed, I felt panicked. My heart was racing and I couldn't get a breath.

Something was wrong. Very wrong. Then I placed it. There was no sound. Absolutely none. No snap of the sail in the wind or creak from the ropes in the metal cleats. The seagulls weren't making their barking laugh. I opened my mouth and screamed until my throat burned.

Not a sound.

She didn't say anything and she didn't touch me. I knew she was there, because I sensed her. I turned around slowly. She was standing at the back of the boat. Her long hair was blowing in the wind. She held out her arms as if she expected me to run into her embrace. She was bundled up with thick socks and a jacket. We stood there staring at each other for what seemed like forever. I said her name, Evelyn, but the sound never left my mouth. I took a step closer to her and she fell back, stiff as a board, off the boat. I raced to the edge and looked over. She was slowly sinking, her arms and legs out. Her hair was mixing with the strings of seaweed. She looked straight into my eyes. It seemed to me that she didn't look scared or panicked, but rather that she was somehow worried for me. She looked concerned and sad. I reached for her, but it was too far, and as the water soaked her clothes she began sinking faster. Then she was gone. Bubbles rose to the surface while I watched, helpless to do anything.

Suddenly her hands shot out of the water and grabbed me by the wrists. I tumbled into the ice-cold ocean. I opened my mouth and the water rushed in.

I woke up, barely able to choke off the scream that was about to rise from my throat. I sat straight up in bed. My T-shirt was stuck to me with sweat. I wanted to turn on the light, but I was terrified that if I pulled my hands out from under the covers, Evelyn's clammy hand would grab me. Or I could turn on the light and she would be standing by the window again. I took quick, shallow breaths, trying to pull my shit together. I never used to have nightmares. Or if I did they were the typical being naked while taking an exam type. The kind of bad dream where as soon as you wake up you know you're fine. Instead I was still shaking and couldn't get rid of the feeling that I was in trouble. What was I going to do, sit there terrified until morning?

Actually, staying awake wasn't a half-bad idea. I shot a look at the clock and saw it was two a.m. Four hours until six. That wasn't too bad, a measly four hours. Heck, once Anita and I waited outside a music store for nine hours for concert tickets. That was outside where there had been bums, and Anita was pretty sure she saw a rat by the Dumpster. It could have been rabid. If I could wait nine hours there, why wouldn't I be able to make it a lousy four hours comfy in my own bed? I would just sit right here until it started to get light. It's well known that things that go bump in the night can be under your bed, but they aren't allowed in. It's some sort of rule. As long as I stayed under the covers, nothing could touch me. Besides, now there were only three hours and fifty-eight minutes to go. The time was practically flying by. I tried to distract myself by doing the times tables in my head.

I made it until the threes before a new problem, in addition to my possible haunting, came up. I had to pee. Three hours fifty-two minutes. I tried crossing my legs and thinking dry desert thoughts. I wasn't going to make it until six a.m. No way. That left me two choices:

1. Stay here and pee the bed. This option was fraught with a whole load of downsides, not the least being forced to sit in a puddle of my own urine for hours (three hours forty-seven minutes to be exact). Then there would be the morning humiliation to consider. Dick's great-grandmother probably made this bed by collecting feathers off her pet goose. He would shit if I peed in it. He would make me sleep on rubber sheets as long as I lived here. Plus Nathaniel would know. I would be his spastic stepsister with an incontinence problem.

2. Leave the bed and make a run for the bathroom. This had the upside of not getting me a year's subscription to Bedwetters Anonymous. The downside was obvious. I had to leave the safety of the covers and risk the dead girl grabbing ahold of me.

I made it another three minutes by crossing my legs in a complicated yoga position I didn't know I could make. When I couldn't stand it anymore, I reached out as fast as I could and yanked the chain on my bedside lamp. The light clicked on, and no one touched me. I counted to three and opened my eyes. The room was empty. On the window seat Mr. Stripes the stuffed zebra was propped up where I'd left him.

"Stop staring at me." I was glad he didn't do what I said. He kept sitting there doing nothing the way a proper unanimated stuffed animal should. My breathing started to slow down. I was almost 100 percent certain I was alone. I jumped out of bed (on the off chance Evelyn's hands would shoot out from under the bed and grab my ankles) and did the dance to the bathroom. Ah, sweet relief!

I drank some water from the bathroom sink and then rubbed my wet hands over my face. It was just a bad dream. A freaky, creepy, lay-off-the-Oreos-after-ten kind of dream, but that was it. Nightmares are common. In science class last year we'd learned that 50 percent of adults have occasional nightmares. Fifty percent. That's like a majority. Or it would be a majority if some of the other 50 percent admitted that they did too. I was going to go back in there, crawl into bed, and drift back off to sleep. This time I would dream about something happy. I'd heard that if you were concentrating on something when you fell asleep, you could make yourself dream about that topic. I'd focus on happy thoughts. My thoughts were going to be Technicolor Disney-princess happy. Singing bluebirds, dancing chipmunks, fa la la la.

I was almost back to bed when I stepped on something sharp and felt it snap and crunch under my foot. I sucked a breath in through my teeth. I plopped down on the bed and pulled up my leg. There was a thin line of blood on the ball of my foot. I looked down at the floor, trying to figure out what I'd stepped on.

There, next to the bed, was a small pile of seashells. One of the larger shells, pink and brown, was broken into thirds.

Chapter 17

"What did you do with the seashells?"

"Are you kidding me? Who cares what I did with the shells? The important part is that they were there at all. I'm sure they weren't there when I went to bed, but after I had the ocean ghost dream, they were there. Seashells do not wander in on their own. They don't even have feet."

"You didn't throw them away, did you?" Anita asked.

I chewed on my thumbnail. I'd made a regular three-course meal out of my fingernails today. I started with an appetizer of pinkie nail, rounded out the meal with the filling—and satisfying—index nail, and was capping off today's anxiety keratin feast with my thumb.

"I didn't throw them away. Should I?" I kicked myself for asking Anita for advice. She was the kind of person who would come up with some sort of elaborate ritual that would require me to burn the shells on a mountaintop while in the middle of a lunar eclipse or something.

"No. Definitely not. The shells are a message."

"Why couldn't she just send a freaking text? Or take out an ad in the local paper?"

"Tell me you are not mocking the spirit world. How much bad karma do you need? Maybe later you could go kick some puppies or a nun or something. Jeez." Anita gave a disgusted sigh.

"What kind of messages are a nightmare and a pile of seashells?"

"I don't know, but she's clearly trying to say something."

"Maybe she wants me to get out of her room."

"I doubt it. I can't see a spirit being that hung up on who's living in her bedroom. I bet she wants you to figure out what happened. Avenge-her-death kind of thing."

"Avenge her death? Does she think I'm some sort of teen version of Chuck Norris?"

"I doubt it. I suspect you're the best she's got to work with."

I was lying on my bed with my feet pressed against the wall. I was picking at the fluff on top of Mr. Stripes's head while we talked.

"I can only imagine how disappointed she must be to be stuck with me as her avenger."

"Skip your insecurity mantra. I think you should hold the shells while you meditate, and maybe she'll send you another message."

"I don't want another message. I want her to go away and leave me alone. I've got enough of my own issues to deal with; I don't need to take on her stuff."

"The quickest way to get rid of her is to listen to what she's trying to say. Give the kid a break—she's dead. If she didn't have some kind of brain injury when she was alive, maybe she could tell you more clearly what she wants now. It's not exactly her fault that death didn't improve her communication skills."

"What if it's not a message? What if it's something worse?"

"Worse? What makes you think a message is a bad thing? You're so lucky. She chose you from the beyond. Nothing like that ever happens to me. I could live on top of a desecrated Indian burial ground and no one would haunt me."

"What if I'm not being haunted?" I held my breath waiting for her to answer.

"Oh, no you don't. Don't even go there."

"Go where?"

"You're worried you've snapped. Taken a one-way trip down the wacky expressway. Shopping for the sweaters where the arms tie behind you. Crazy train."

"You've got a huge career ahead of you as a social worker. You've got such a gentle bedside manner." I acted like I was annoyed even though I was actually relieved. If Anita thought I really was going crazy, she would never joke about it. "If you ever need a recommendation so you can get a job as a counselor, let me know."

"BFF manifesto rule number one: no bullshit. If I thought you were insane, I'd tell you."

"You have to admit it's a lot more likely that I'm crazy than that there's a ghost trying to send me a message."

"No. You think it's more likely because you're a skeptic. Besides, just because your dad went crazy doesn't mean you will."

"But I could." I took a deep breath. "Thank God you're coming to visit this weekend. I've got tons of stuff planned. You can help me figure out what to do with the shells then, okay?"

Anita didn't say anything. Uh-oh. She wasn't exactly the silent type.

"You are coming this weekend, right?" We'd been organizing this visit since before I even moved. It wouldn't be too much of an exaggeration to say I'd been counting down the minutes.

"There's this thing."

"Thing?" My stomach fell to the floor.

"Kat is having a party on Saturday."

"Kat has a party every week."

"Yeah, but her parents are out of town and she's doing this beach theme. Everybody's going. Including Ryan. He made a point of asking me if I was going."

Anita had a weakness for Ryan. She'd been in love with him since eighth grade. She was smart about a lot of things, but Ryan was her Kryptonite. When he was around I could actually see IQ points leaking out of her ears. Anita had been chasing him since the gym class when he spiked a volleyball that hit her right in the face. She went down with a huge geyser of a bloody nose. When she came to, Ryan was leaning over her. She figured that made him her hero. She seemed to fail to notice that he was the one who drilled the ball right at her nose in the first place. While Anita liked Ryan, Ryan liked that Anita liked him. He had a sixth sense that allowed him to tell when she was finally getting ready to move on, and then he would suddenly start flirting with her all over again. Nothing ever came of it, but it didn't stop Anita from going back for more.

"I thought you wanted to see this place," I reminded her.

"I do. I really do. It's just that this might not be the best weekend. I could come some other time."

"Dick and my mom are all 'this is not a hotel' about people coming to visit. They don't want people just dropping by. That's why we planned this." I could tell I was whining, but I didn't care. She'd promised to come.

"Dick's a dick."

"Trust me, I know. I'm living the full twenty-four/seven Dick experience." I sighed. "I'll talk to my mom and see if she'll let me come over there. She's been focused on how we have to spend time as a family, but I bet she'll give in on this. She knows how much I was looking forward to seeing you. Maybe your mom could pick me up at the ferry."

"Uh. That's the thing."

I could feel my ears getting hot. I chewed on the side of my mouth. "You don't want me to come to your place? Are you afraid I'm going to cramp your style with Ryan?"

"No." She hesitated. I bet Sharon the court jester was encouraging her to throw herself at Ryan. "My mom is hosting a fund-raising party for my brother's football team."

"So? I used to hang out at your house all the time. Your mom invited me to live with you."

"I'm just telling you what she said. She doesn't want extra people around."

"Extra people. That's great. Now I'm extra. I hope you and Kat have a great time at the party."

"That's not fair. Do you expect me to sit around by myself? You're the one who moved."

"I didn't move. My mom moved and made me go with her." I paced back and forth with my phone.

"So now I'm supposed to feel sorry for you? You're living in a mansion with the hottest guy in the world just down the hall, and, oh yeah, you're a cheerleader."

"I never asked to live here. The mansion is haunted, the hottest guy in the world likes my friend Nicole, and, oh yeah, I might as well be a cheerleader because it's not like I can count on you to keep me busy." Anita started to say something else, but I cut her off. "And another thing? Ryan doesn't like you. The closest you two will get to making out is him fucking with your head."

Anita hung up without saying another word. I clicked my phone off and threw it on the bed. Then I burst into tears.

Chapter 18

"We could do pedicures," Jenni suggested.

"I don't have any nail polish," I admitted.

Brit's eyes went as wide as if I had declared that I didn't like to keep food and water in the house. I had the sense Brit was one of those girls who has a tackle box full of makeup, the kind that opens up with an accordion of shelves stuffed with potions and lotions and weighs at least a hundred pounds. I was willing to bet Brit had an entire bathroom shelf full of every shade of nail polish and could rattle off their goofy names, like Tomato Kiss Sunrise, by memory.

"I could check and see if my mom has any," I offered, even though the idea of having to touch someone else's feet grossed me out. I wasn't against a good pedicure, but where I lived, you went to the nail salon for that kind of thing, where only trained professionals were allowed to scrape the dead skin off your feet. It wasn't something you asked your friends to do.

I hadn't had a slumber party since I was a kid, and based on how this was going so far, I figured it was going to be my last one. Brit, Sam, Jenni, and Nicole were sitting on my bedroom floor, and I could tell they were bored. When Anita would come over and spend the night, we never seemed to run out of things to talk about. We'd be up all night laughing and joking. With this group, we couldn't seem to come up with a single thing to talk about. At this rate, we were going to be reduced to the strange small talk you have with elderly relatives: favorite subject at school or what you plan to study in college. I couldn't blame them for not wanting to be here. *I* didn't want to be here, but since it was my house, there was no way I could leave. I glanced over at the clock. It was only ten p.m., which seemed a bit early to suggest that we call it a night and go to sleep. I wondered if Dick kept any board games other than Scrabble in the house.

"I know what we can do." Nicole got up and began rummaging through the duffel bag she'd brought. She pulled out a flat board and then flipped it over so we could all see it was a Ouija board. She shook it back and forth.

"I don't know," Jenni said. "I'm not sure that's a good idea. I mean, here." She looked over at me and blushed. "Sorry."

I shrugged. How could I be mad when I was thinking the same thing? Playing with a Ouija board in this house seemed like running through a tinder-dry forest playing with a flamethrower.

Bad plan. Maybe later we could try juggling carving knives or swim with sharks while wearing fish suits.

"Don't be a scaredy-cat." Nicole plunked back down and put the board right in the middle of our circle.

"Wait a minute. I think Jenni's right," I said.

"I think it would be fun," Brit insisted, scooching up closer to the board. I did my best not to roll my eyes. Brit would agree with any plan Nicole had, up to and including the cliché of jumping off a bridge.

"Sam? What do you think? You aren't scared, are you?" Nicole asked. Sam looked back and forth between all of us.

"It might be fun," Sam said slowly, sounding like she thought it would be as much fun as being dragged naked through a pile of broken glass. From what I knew of her so far, though, she had the spine of an earthworm; no way was she going to stand up to Nicole.

"Majority wins!" Nicole declared. She dropped the plastic triangle onto the board. "Okay, everyone touch their fingers lightly on the planchette."

"I really don't want to do this," I said.

Nicole leaned back and crossed her arms. "It's your place. What *do* you want to do?"

My brain scrambled to come up with something. "We could watch a movie," I suggested.

"I thought you didn't have any DVDs," Brit reminded me.

"We could see what's on cable." It wasn't my fault that this crappy island didn't have a decent rental store. Back home in

Seattle I didn't have to buy DVDs. We could rent or download them like normal people. "Or we could play some other kind of game."

"A rousing game of Monopoly. That sounds exciting," Brit said with a snort. "Maybe later we could play with our Barbies or pretend to be veterinarians with your stuffed toys."

My eyes narrowed. She shouldn't be messing with Mr. Stripes. Making fun of a girl for her plush zebra was hitting below the belt. "Fine. Let's play." I put my fingers on the planchette.

Sam, Brit, and Nicole joined me. Jenni shook her head when we looked at her. She sat hugging her knees. Nicole closed her eyes, and Brit immediately did the same.

"Spirit world, hear our voices. Join us now," Nicole said in a low voice.

Nothing happened. "Aren't we supposed to ask a specific question or something?" Sam asked.

"It's polite to give them the chance to talk first," Nicole huffed as if she were the Miss Manners of the undead.

The tips of my fingers started to tingle. The planchette began to quiver. It slid slowly over to where the numbers were listed across the top.

"It's moving!" Brit hissed, in case the rest of us were incapable of noticing it for ourselves.

The planchette hovered over the number one, then slid to the number two, paused, and then went to the number three and stopped.

"So it's just counting?" Brit asked.

The planchette shook and repeated the number sequence. This time faster. Our eyes met over the board. No one said anything, and we waited to see what would happen. Then it repeated the numbers again.

"Spirit, can you tell us who you are?" Nicole asked.

123

123

123

123

I didn't know much about the afterlife, but so far it seemed like those in the spirit world tended to repeat themselves.

"What is the point of this?" Brit grumped. "Let's ask it something."

"What do the numbers mean?" I asked. The triangle didn't move.

"Ask something interesting. Who will I marry?" Brit tried.

The triangle didn't move. It looked like Brit was headed for spinsterhood. I kept that thought to myself, since she didn't look like the kind of person who could handle the truth.

"Spirit, can you tell me? Who is my destiny?" Nicole asked.

The triangle didn't move at first, but then it began to slide across the board. I noticed this time that there was no tingling in my fingers. It felt different somehow.

The planchette slid over to the *N*, pausing for a beat, and then moved toward the *A*. I looked up from the board to Nicole.

She was smiling. I glanced back down. I couldn't tell for certain, but it seemed to me that her fingers looked tense. She was moving it. I was sure of it. I knew exactly what it was about to spell out. I pressed my fingers down a bit more firmly, and the triangle paused, unable to finish its journey to the *T*. Nicole's eyebrows crunched together. I could feel her trying to pull it forward without looking as if she was doing it.

"What's it trying to say?" Sam asked.

Nicole and I were locked in a fierce battle of finger strength. Our eyes met. The planchette shook underneath all our fingers. She would pull it closer to the *T* and I would pull it back. No way was she going to spell out Nathaniel as her destiny.

"Anyone else notice how cold it's getting in here?" Jenni said. She rubbed her hands up and down her arms.

"It is cold," Sam said. "Check it out, I can practically see my breath in here."

"Would you focus?" Nicole snapped.

The tingling returned to my fingertips. In fact it moved passed a tingling. It felt like a low-level electrical shock. Sam hissed and pulled her fingers back. The planchette began shaking, then bouncing on the board. Suddenly it shot out from under our fingers and flew against the wall. We all jumped back.

"What the hell was that?" Brit asked, her voice sounding high and screechy.

"There's something here," Nicole intoned, her voice low. "Can you feel it?"

I wanted to say no, but my tongue was completely dry. I could feel something, and I was certain it wasn't anything Nicole was doing. The room felt like there was an electrical charge in the air, as if lightning were suddenly going to break out in the middle of my bedroom.

BANG!

We all jumped and whirled around to face my bathroom. The door to the bathroom was closed, but it sounded like someone had kicked the tub.

BANG BANG.

Jenni looked like she wanted to cry. Brit had her hands over her mouth.

BANG BANG BANG.

It was quiet for a beat. I was just about to say something, but then it started again. *BANG. BANG BANG. BANG BANG BANG.*

"It's counting again. One, two, three," Nicole said. Her face had gone white.

"Make it stop," Brit said to me.

"I'm not doing anything," I said, pointing out the obvious.

BANG. BANG BANG. BANG BANG BANG.

Even Nicole looked shaken now. "Someone should go check it out." The rest of the group looked at me. Figures. It might be my place, but talking to the dead hadn't been my idea. Why was it no one expected Nicole to do any ghost busting?

I stood up. The banging stopped. I took a couple of shuffling steps toward the bathroom, but it stayed quiet. I could hear the girls breathing heavily behind me. My hand reached out. I hesitated before touching the doorknob. My heart was hammering a thousand beats per second. I made myself count to five, and then I grabbed the knob.

I flung the door open. I saw the mirror directly in front of me; only, instead of my own reflection, it flashed Evelyn's face. Her hands were squeezing either side of her face, and her mouth was open in a scream. The mirror fell off the wall and shattered on the floor. Everyone screamed.

Chapter 19

Sam kept screaming. I stood in the door of the bathroom staring at where the mirror used to be. There was a *plink* as a piece of glass slid down in the sink. Pieces of my reflection lay in the broken shards on the floor. I could hear someone running up the stairs toward my room.

Jenni jumped up from the floor and bolted. She flung open the bedroom door and ran straight into someone. She started screaming again and swinging her arms wildly.

"Hey, easy." Nathaniel grabbed her arms. She was still screaming. He held her by the shoulders and shook her. Her screams cut off when she realized who had her and she began to cry. She backed up and collapsed onto the window seat.

"Oh, Nathaniel, thank God." Nicole flew across the room and threw herself into his arms.

"What happened?" Nathaniel stood there with his arms out while Nicole clung to his chest. He saw me, and then something else caught his eye. "You're bleeding."

I followed his gaze down and saw a shard of the mirror sticking out of the top of my foot. A slick of blood was pooling on the floor. Nathaniel pulled Nicole off of him and passed her to Brit. He went down on one knee in front me as if he were about to propose.

"What is going on in here?" Dick burst through the door. Jenni and Sam were both crying to beat the band.

I opened my mouth to try to explain, but at that moment Nathaniel yanked the glass out of my foot and I let out a yelp instead. Nathaniel grabbed the box of Kleenex next to the bed and pressed a wad of tissues down on the cut. He handed me the mirror shard.

Nicole took a step forward and kicked the Ouija board under my bed before Dick could see it. "We were goofing around and the bathroom mirror broke." She gave Dick a sweet, innocent smile, and when he looked around the room, she glared at the rest of us. Brit managed to pull it together first. She scrambled up off the floor and stood next to Nicole.

"I guess the sound of the glass breaking scared us," Brit said. She nudged Jenni, who was still crying on the window seat. Sam let out a shrill laugh that sounded way more manic than reassuring.

"How did you break the mirror? Were you playing football up

here? We could hear you banging around all the way downstairs." Dick gave one of his hearty fake chuckles.

Nicole pressed her palm on Dick's chest. "Oh, Mr. Wickham, playing football?" She laughed as if that was so silly she could hardly stand it. Nicole had a booming future as a society wife ahead of her. Ass kissing was an Olympic sport for her.

Dick looked at me and waited to hear my explanation. I didn't like the idea of going along with Nicole, but admitting we were playing with a Ouija board wasn't going to make the situation better. I shrugged and looked away.

"I think you're going to need stitches," Nathaniel said. "This cut is pretty deep. Do you want me to take you?"

"I want to go home," Jenni said. Her lower lip was shaking and she wasn't able to look directly at Nicole or Dick. "I don't feel well."

"Me neither," Sam squeaked.

"Maybe we'd better call it a night," I mumbled. I guess I didn't have to worry any more about how to spend the rest of my slumber party. Jenni and Sam started grabbing their things off the floor and stuffing them into their bags.

"I could go with you to the clinic," Nicole offered. I wasn't stupid enough to imagine for a second that she cared about my foot. She would spend all her time throwing herself back into Nathaniel's arms.

"I'll get my keys and meet you downstairs." Nathaniel stood. His sweatpants had a dark maroon splotch of blood on the knee.

Dick brushed past me as if I weren't even standing there and looked into the bathroom. "I'll get your mom to come up and clean the room."

"I can do it," I mumbled. "Nicole, you don't need to come, but maybe you could give everyone else a ride home?"

"That would be great," Dick agreed, clapping Nicole on the back.

Nicole's mouth pressed shut. She had no interest in being everyone's chauffeur, but there wasn't any easy way to refuse.

I pulled on my oversize gray sweater and rummaged in my drawer for a pair of thick socks while the girls gathered their things. I managed to get my socks on, but a red bloom immediately appeared over the cut on my foot. I stuffed a few handfuls of tissues into my sock to stanch the bleeding. Then we filed out quietly, Dick following us down the stairs.

"Everyone's leaving?" my mom said, coming out from the kitchen. She looked confused.

"There was a bit of roughhousing and a mirror got broken," Dick said, taking the glass of wine from my mom's hand. "A few of the girls are feeling a bit shaken up."

My mom looked down, noticing the bloodstain on my sock. "Isobel?"

"It's nothing," Dick said. "Nathaniel's going to take her down to the clinic and get it checked out."

"I'll get my purse."

Dick caught her by the arm and pulled her close. "No need

for everyone to decamp on me. The cut's not bad. Nathaniel can handle it. If there's a problem, he'll give us a call."

"Do you want me to come?" My mom rested a cool hand on my arm.

"Come on, now. The girl is seventeen, not seven. There's no need to treat her like she's a baby," Dick said. He ruffled my hair like I was a scrappy Irish setter. "She's all grown up."

I wasn't sure if I wanted my mother to come or not, but I was sure I didn't want Dick making the decision.

Nathaniel's car pulled up in front of the house. Nicole and the rest of the group moved past me, mumbling their good-byes.

I realized I was still holding the piece of mirror that had been in my foot. The point was sharp, but the sides were dull. I turned it over in my hand, the light from the wall sconces bouncing off its surface. There was a perfect circle from a blood drop in the center. My thumb rubbed across it. I blinked. It looked like the reflective qualities of the glass must have been ruined somehow in the break; the surface looked almost smoky gray in parts. I lifted the shard closer and gasped. There was a black-and-white image in the glass, just a fragment, but I was sure it was part of the image of Evelyn's face I'd seen. It was as if a part of her image had imprinted itself like a photograph onto the glass.

Before I could think about it further, I slid the piece of mirror into my pocket and slipped out into the night to join Nathaniel.

Chapter 20

It was confirmed. There was no doubt about it now. I was crazy. Proof was staring at me in the mirror. I yanked down on the bottom of the cheerleading sweater, trying to force it to be longer, but as soon as I let go, it popped back up, exposing a two-inch gap between it and my skirt. That is, if you could call this a skirt. It looked more like a pleated scarf I had tied tightly around my waist. Also, in the interest of full disclosure, it wasn't really a gap between the sweater and the skirt: there was a distinct roll of flesh filling all available space. It was like a ring of raw Pillsbury biscuit dough circled my entire waist, squeezed up from the tight waistband of the skirt. What was this uniform anyway? A size zero?

I'd thought I was in shape before I'd squeezed into this outfit, which looked like it was tailored to fit a fifth grader, but now

I felt sick at the thought of wearing it anywhere. Suddenly I understood how people developed body issues. I normally like my curves, but now they seemed a bit too much. I tried to stand up straighter while holding my breath. That was better, except for the fact that sooner or later I was going to need air. I might have been crazy to think I could pull this look off, but at least it was the right kind of crazy. You never see crazy cheerleaders. Perky. Annoying. Occasionally slutty, but almost never clinically crazy.

I couldn't believe I'd let Nicole talk me into this. What was I thinking? There are cheerleader types. People who are genetically gifted since birth to look good in these outfits and who actually want to stand in front of groups of people and yell out things like:

We're the Cougars
And we can't be beat.
We've got the power
To knock you off your feet!

I am not one of the genetically chosen. Bad poetry yelled in an arena was still bad poetry. The past two weeks had done nothing but convince me I was cheerleader material. I didn't want to be a cheerleader, but I did want to have friends on this island, and so far Nicole was the only one who seemed interested. Nicole was the kind who associated friendship and cheerleading as pretty much the same thing. Having her as a friend was my ticket to surviving this year, and, without Anita, I desperately needed a friend. I wasn't fooling myself. I knew Nicole was using me, but in fairness, I was using her to avoid leper status. It seemed a fairly even deal.

It had already been two weeks, and no one in the group had mentioned my slumber party. It was as if we had signed some sort of nondisclosure agreement or the event had never happened. In the end, I hadn't even needed stitches. The clinic had cleaned my foot and closed the wound with one of those butterfly Band-Aids. The piece of mirror was wrapped up in a sheet of paper and buried deep in the underwear drawer of my dresser.

I pulled on the sweater again and watched it creep upward. Maybe it didn't look as bad as I feared. I could kick myself for making fun when Anita bought Spanx. I told her we were too young to wear a girdle. I would give up my as-of-yet-unborn first child to have a girdle on hand now. I sighed. I looked stupid and I had no choice. I had to go to school like this. Ever since Nicole had taken me under her wing, suddenly I could do no wrong. When I walked into a classroom, there was always someone saving a seat for me. Random strangers complimented me on things like my hair. I might have been imagining it, but it seemed like even the teachers liked me better. If I raised my hand, they always called on me, and no matter what I said, they would always reply, "*What a great answer!*" Either I had gotten smarter (doubtful) or there was some sort of halo effect from being a part of the sacred circle. Yesterday after school it was made official. I was given my own uniform. I was a cheerleader. Just in time for the pep rally.

I went downstairs and paused just a moment outside the kitchen. I could hear everyone inside. I considered skipping breakfast, but I figured I might as well get it all over with at once. I pushed the door open and headed straight for the refrigerator without looking around.

"Well, look at you." Dick gave a wolf whistle.

Uh. Creepy.

"Isobel?" My mom was holding the milk carton and staring at me in shock. She acted like I had wandered into the kitchen wearing a giant plush mouse costume or some other completely shocking ensemble.

"I'm on the cheerleading squad." I crossed my arms over my chest. I couldn't look at Nathaniel. Could he tell I was one deep breath away from busting out of the seams, or was the sweater tight enough that my boobs had finally caught his attention?

"Really? For the school?" Mom asked.

"No, Mom. I'm a cheerleader for the local animal shelter. *Go neuter!* Of course for the school."

"All the popular girls are on the squad," Nathaniel added. The three of us looked at him. He popped the rest of his slice of toast into his mouth. "Least, that's what I've heard," he added with a slight spray of crumbs.

"This is wonderful." Mom crossed the kitchen and gave me a hug. She was acting like I'd found a cure for some sort of deforming disease. I hadn't seen her this happy since Dick gave her the baseball-size diamond ring.

"It's not a big deal." I grabbed the orange juice and poured myself a glass. "I still can't do a decent cartwheel. I only got on the squad because my friend Nicole is the captain."

"Don't underestimate yourself. Wickhams are winners," Dick said.

"I'm not a Wickham," I pointed out, tossing back the OJ like it was a shot of tequila.

"I was a cheerleader in high school," my mom said, her voice all dreamy. "Some of my favorite memories are from that time."

"We'll have to get Isobel to lend you her outfit. I'd love to see you as a cheerleader," Dick said with a leer.

Nathaniel and I shared a look of disgust. I could have gone my entire life without the image of my mom and Dick engaged in a sexual role-playing game. Especially in *my* clothes.

"You're terrible, Richard." My mom giggled and whacked Dick with a dish towel. I would have whacked him harder with the cutting board, but that was just my preference. She turned her attention back to me. "I'm proud of you, honey. This is a positive thing to have in your life. I'm glad to see you moving in the right direction."

I frowned. "I wasn't aware I was going in the wrong direction."

"Don't get all bristly. All I meant is that cheerleading is better for you than art."

"You think art's bad for me?"

"I think spending all your time on your own isn't good for you. Art is solitary, all that time spent in your head. It's important, given your family history, for you to make nice, healthy social relationships."

I could see Nathaniel raise an eyebrow at her comment. I slammed my juice glass down in the sink. I whirled around and bolted out of the room. I made it outside before my mom caught up to me. She grabbed me by the elbow.

"What in the world is wrong with you?"

"I can't believe you said that. My 'family history'? Did you tell Dick about my dad?"

"Richard's my husband. I don't have secrets from him."

"He's nothing to *me*." I could hear the tears in my voice, and at the same time, I was so angry I could barely speak. "He has no right to know my personal business."

She touched my arm. "Honey, you're making a mountain out of a molehill. Richard cares about you. You don't need to be embarrassed; he's your family now too."

"Just because you married him doesn't make him my family," I pointed out.

"I do not understand your irrational dislike of him. Tell me one thing he's done to you."

I couldn't explain why I didn't like Dick. There wasn't something I could point to, but he felt slick to me, like a politician. Someone who shook your hand and smiled, not because he liked you, but because he had something to gain.

Mom tapped her foot impatiently. "Blaming Richard because you didn't want to move isn't fair to him. Blaming me for talking with him about my concerns also isn't fair."

I felt like screaming in frustration. "What about being fair to me? If you're concerned, why don't you talk to me about it?"

"I do talk to you. You simply don't want to listen. Ever since we moved here you've been moody, having these wild dreams, talking about all these conspiracy theories with murder and family curses."

"I'm not going crazy."

"You should know that is exactly what Dick says when I tell him I'm worried. He says all of this is just a normal teenage response to all this change."

I chewed on the inside of my lip. I hated that Dick was sticking up for me. "So I suppose Nathaniel knows too? Maybe you could take an ad out in the *Nairne News* and tell the whole world that I'm on the edge."

"The only person I've talked to is Richard, and I talk with him because I care. These mood swings you have concern me." She tried to tuck a strand of hair behind my ear, but I brushed her hand away.

"I'm having mood swings because you picked me up and moved me here to the middle of nowhere so you could have what *you* wanted. I *never* wanted the same things you wanted. I couldn't care less about this big house, or Dick's money, or this stupid cheerleading skirt. Just because you don't understand my perspective, don't act like what I want is crazy."

"What do you want from me, Isobel?" My mom's lower lip was shaking, but I refused to feel sorry for her. She created this situation, and now I was supposed to believe I was the bad guy?

"I want you to leave me alone." I didn't wait to see what else she had to say. I turned around and walked away.

Chapter 21

My goal was to get through the assembly without throwing up, falling over, or forgetting the words to our routine. I just wanted the whole thing to be over. Our football team, the mighty Cougars, was leaving on the next ferry for a game, and it was our job to appropriately pump them up for the upcoming battle. The rest of the squad would go with them to the game, but as the official alternate I didn't merit a ticket off the island, just to the humiliation of the pep rally.

We were in the gym. The students in the bleachers were giving at least a halfhearted effort to look like they were infused with school spirit, because assembly was at least marginally better than sitting in class. Principal Hoffman cleared his throat and gripped the sides of the lectern. He was at least six and half feet tall and as bald as Mr. Clean.

"A new year provides new opportunities," he intoned. "A winning season. A championship." He looked across the bleachers. I was getting the feeling that Principal Hoffman had a bit of a Churchill complex. "But let me be clear: a new opportunity is not the same as a fresh start. Our past cannot be left behind. History has a long memory. It grips us. It holds on." Hoffman held out his clenched hands for those who weren't grasping just how tenacious history could be without a visual aid. "We can't forget our history with the Spartans. I can assure you they haven't forgotten. They think they can beat us, but what they don't know is that we haven't forgotten either. The ghosts of our former teams will be on that field with us tonight. We won't repeat the past. We'll learn from it. We will take what we know and use it to beat them!"

Hoffman pounded the lectern with his palm. The crowd gave a cheer.

"Who are we?" Hoffman bellowed.

"Cougars!" the crowd yelled back. Brit jammed her elbow in my side, and I realized the rest of the cheerleaders were standing and shaking their pom-poms.

"Cougars!" I yelled out a beat after everyone else. Nicole shot me a disapproving look.

"Okay, we're up," Jenni whispered. She and Sam plastered perfectly matched pageant girl smiles on their faces and bounced out onto the floor in tandem. I swallowed hard and followed them. No guts, no glory.

Ms. Lancaster turned on our music. The bass was turned up so hard I could feel it pounding in my chest.

"Ready? Okay!" Nicole yelled out, and we began our routine. I could hear people yelling and cheering as we went, so we must have been doing okay. We spun around, bent down, and looked out at the crowd through our split legs.

Suddenly Nathaniel was pushing his way down the stairs and out onto the floor. He pushed past Sam and grabbed me.

"Hey!" I yanked my arm back. "What are you doing? We're in the middle of a routine." Ms. Lancaster cut off the music. I could feel my face flush red-hot in embarrassment.

"You're flashing your underwear to the entire school," Nathaniel said under his breath.

I rolled my eyes. "It's not my underwear. It's the bottom that goes with the cheerleading skirt." I flipped the skirt up to show him the white cotton bottoms with orange and black polka dots, the school colors. I heard someone in the crowd let out a whoop.

Nathaniel grabbed Jenni's skirt and flipped it up. Her bottom was solid black Lycra.

I shook my head in confusion. "This is the uniform they gave me."

The rest of the squad was huddled together. I could see Nicole pressing her lips together to keep a smile from breaking out.

"It's a joke. Sort of a hazing thing we do to anyone new on the squad," she said. Brit choked off a laugh; even Sam and Jenni were smirking.

I looked out at the crowd. Tons of people in the audience were laughing. Dear God. I had just stood in front of the entire school and shaken my ass in giant polka-dotted granny panties.

"Not funny," Nathaniel said, glaring at Nicole.

"I didn't think she would wear them," Nicole explained, but she could barely smother her giggles. "I figured she would know those weren't the right bottoms."

"How would I know? I've never cheered before." I blinked back tears.

"Girls? We're in the middle of a routine here," Ms. Lancaster said. "Take your places." She gave a brittle smile to the crowd and a nod to Mr. Hoffman to show she had everything under control.

"Isobel, I'm sorry," Nicole apologized, suddenly all sincere. "It was a joke. I didn't mean to embarrass you. I feel terrible." She was talking to me, but the whole time she was looking at Nathaniel.

"You didn't embarrass me. You humiliated me." I wanted to spit in her face. This is what I got for thinking I could pull off being a cheerleader, for thinking any of these people were really my friends. The only reason Nicole hung out with me was to be near Nathaniel. I thought having a lousy friend was better than being completely alone, but I was beginning to suspect I was wrong. I swallowed to keep from bursting into tears.

"Girls. Pull it together," Ms. Lancaster hissed from the sidelines. She motioned to someone standing near the sound system.

"Screw this." You couldn't pay me enough to stay there and

do the whole thing again. I ran for the door. The music started up again, chasing me out, and I could hear Nicole start the cheer from the top.

The hallway was mercifully empty. For good measure, I kicked one of the lockers as hard as I could. When it didn't beg for mercy, I gave it a few extra kicks, as well as calling it a few choice names.

"You okay?"

I whirled around, and Nathaniel was standing there watching me.

"The entire school saw."

"Could have been worse."

"Really?" I said in my most incredulous voice. "How do you figure?"

"Could have been thong panties." Nathaniel shoved his hair out of his eyes. "Besides, you looked good. If you have to flash the world, at least look good doing it."

Did he just compliment my ass? Did this mean he noticed I even had an ass?

"I should have known better. I'm not cheerleader material." I pulled the sweater down for the millionth time that day. "I never even wanted to be a cheerleader."

"So why did you do it?"

"I don't know. This place is different. I don't fit in." I looked him in the eye. "Not that fitting in is a big deal to me. It just seemed easier to go with the flow, try out a different perspective for the year."

"So you tried cheerleading as a social experiment?"

"Exactly. Of course, I ended up just looking stupid." I bit my lip and averted my eyes.

"Better than looking bitchy like Nicole."

"You think Nicole's a bitch?" I rubbed my nose and didn't meet his eyes.

"I think what she did was shitty. She should have told you before you went out there."

"I thought you were crazy about her."

Nathaniel laughed. "What made you think that?"

"You're always flirting with her."

"Lately she's around my house. I've just been making small talk."

"It's my house too."

"Fine. She's always in our house."

"So it's a matter of convenience? You flirt with anyone who happens to be in our house?" I asked. Nathaniel shrugged. "You don't flirt with me." As soon as the words fell out of my mouth, I wanted to swallow them back down.

"Would you like me to flirt with you?" Nathaniel's eyes seemed to have me pinned against the lockers.

"No," I said, thinking, *Yes, yes, yes.* "Don't be stupid. I was just making a point."

A cheer came from the gym followed by the sound of people stamping their feet on the bleachers.

"Sounds like the pep rally is over," Nathaniel said.

I glanced at the clock. It was almost noon. I was not looking forward to sitting in the cafeteria while everyone discussed my panty parade and hearing Nicole tell me how the whole thing had been nothing more than good, clean fun while angling for an invitation to come over and drool on Nathaniel. The thought filled me with dread, and I squeezed my eyes shut, tilting my head back to thud against the nearest locker. If only I could make the whole world dissolve away.

"Do you want me to take you home?"

I opened one eye to see if he was being serious. "Skip the rest of the day? We could get into trouble."

"I live for danger. Besides, our reputations practically require us to behave badly."

I smiled at that. "You do come from a cursed family."

"And you've developed a habit of flashing your undies at your fellow schoolmates." He pretended to be horrified. "Dear God, woman, there were freshmen in the audience. Mere children." Nathaniel shook his head sadly.

"Most likely I scarred them for life. The sight of granny panties will probably trigger flashbacks for the rest of their lives."

There was another wave of sound from the gym. Nathaniel held out his hand to me.

"Let's go."

I didn't think about it anymore. I grabbed his hand and we left.

Chapter 22

"How can you not know how to drive?" Nathaniel asked. It was a surprisingly warm day, so he had the windows down. The wind was blowing through my hair.

We were driving around the island in Nathaniel's car. Lots of people have cars that were passed down from family, except usually it's a beat-up Ford Taurus with ripped interior and big rust pimples on the sides. Nathaniel had his grandfather's 1960 Triumph. We realized as soon as we got in the car that we couldn't go home. Dick and my mom were pretty focused on each other, but even they would guess school didn't let out at noon.

"I didn't need to know how to drive in Seattle," I explained. "In civilization there's this concept you may never have heard of called public transportation."

"What is this thing you call transportation?"

I smacked him and rummaged through his lunch bag. He packed a way better lunch than I did. I popped a few of his grapes in my mouth. I dropped one and it rolled under my seat. Shit. Nathaniel kept his car immaculate. I suspected he buffed the leather seats with a soft cloth diaper. I casually leaned over and let my fingers search for the grape, but it was gone. It was going to fester under there until it became a raisin. I leaned back. I better enjoy this ride. Once he knew I left produce to rot in his car, I was going to be back riding my bike.

"Public transportation is better for the environment." I carefully popped another grape into my mouth. "The eco-crowd loves me."

"We already discussed that I'm responsible for global warming, so this adds nothing to the discussion. You must want to know how to drive. The open road. The freedom to go wherever your imagination leads."

"We live on an island. Where am I going to go? Freedom to drive in circles, big deal."

"Are you afraid to drive?" Nathaniel revved the engine as we wound around a corner.

"No, of course not."

Nathaniel stopped in the middle of the road and set the hand brake. "Okay, I'll teach you."

"Now?" I nearly aspirated an entire grape.

"Why not?" Nathaniel opened the door and walked around. He opened my door and bent over as if he were a valet. "Go with the flow."

I called his bluff and walked around to the driver's side. No way was I going to mention that this car cost more than the house I used to live in. If something happened to this car I would have to sell a kidney to pay for the repairs, maybe two. Biology wasn't my best subject, but I was pretty sure I needed to keep at least one. I took my time adjusting the mirrors and seat. I clicked my seat belt and placed my hands on the steering wheel.

"You ready? You're going to place your foot on the clutch, shift the car into first, and slowly let up while at the same time starting to press on the gas. There isn't much traffic around here, so you don't have to worry. Just lightly press on the gas and we're off."

I took a deep breath and did as he instructed. I stepped on the gas and the car shot forward with a roar of the engine. The trees turned to a green blur on either side and Nathaniel let out a high scream. The engine shuddered and the car came to a lurching stop as it stalled. The wayward grape rolled out from under the passenger seat. Nathaniel took a few deep breaths with both hands braced on the console.

"Well, that was interesting," Nathaniel said after a beat. "Here I saw you as a sort of brooding artsy type, and in reality, deep inside you have the heart of a Nascar driver."

"I keep telling you, I'm not any particular type. Your gas pedal is really touchy."

"It's touchy because you stomped on it."

"I didn't stomp." I yanked on the hand brake. "This is stupid. You drive."

"You're going to quit?"

"I'm no good at this. I nearly killed us."

"You aren't allowed to kill us. You realize how that would increase the rumors of my family curse? You can't give up this easy. You know what they say: winners never quit and quitters never win."

"Your dad says that, doesn't he? It has that Wickham home wisdom sound to it."

"That's nothing. You haven't lived until you've been on the receiving end of the 'you're a disappointment to generations of Wickhams' talk. It has subsections dealing with destiny, honor, and the American way."

That surprised me. "How can your dad think you're a disappointment? You're . . ." My voice trailed off because what I'd planned to say was "you're perfect," which might have been a little too honest. "You've got everything going for you," I said instead. "You're smart. And you dress nice."

Nathaniel laughed. "It doesn't matter. Doesn't just about everybody disappoint their parents? They say all they want is for us to be happy, but what they really want is for us to be their do-over. Their second chance at life."

"Don't forget how they want to show you off to their friends and point out what great parents they must be. So if you fail to live up to their standards, not only have you let them down on the do-over, but you've made them look bad to their friends."

"Yeah, but you don't let this stuff get to you like I do," he said.

"What makes you think I don't let it get to me?"

"You do your own thing. You don't try to be a clone of your mom just to make her happy."

"Have you looked at me? I'm wearing a cheerleader outfit. Tell me again how I do my own thing?"

"Fair enough. I expect to see you back to your all black uniform by tomorrow."

"You can count on it." I planned to burn this outfit as soon as I got home.

"You could keep the skirt. It's black."

"And about three inches long," I pointed out.

"Yeah, but you've got the legs for it."

I gave my thighs a whack. "Gams of steal. Comes from all the bike riding and walking I'm doing around here."

"Which brings us back to the car."

"I'm officially hanging up my keys."

"Quitter."

"I'm not a quitter. I just don't want to drive." Nathaniel didn't say anything. He just looked at me. I rubbed my hands on my skirt. "Okay, I don't want to ruin your car."

"This time take your foot off the brake and just let the car roll for a bit. Then we'll try the gas-pedal thing again, nice and slow."

"Why do you want to do this?"

"Isn't it enough for me to thwart the environmentalists' plan by turning another person into a carbon-burning car jockey?"

This time I was the one who didn't say anything.

"Okay, if we're going the honesty route, I want to do something for you. Something nice. This is what I've got," Nathaniel said.

I felt a rush of adrenaline. "Let's do this." I looked over at him. "Does anyone ever call you Nate? Nathaniel's really formal."

"Nathaniel's a family name. I think my dad picked it because it's formal."

I smiled. "So Nate it is." I put the car back into gear and carefully lifted my foot off the brake. The car started rolling slowly forward.

"You got it. Nice and easy this time."

I pressed softly on the gas and the car picked up speed. I was doing it. There wasn't a stall or a shudder. We were going somewhere. We both let out a whoop at the same time.

Chapter 23

I managed to avoid crashing, denting, scratching, or otherwise marring Nate's car all afternoon. There was a close call when a mailbox seemed to jump out in front of me, but I swerved at the last second. Maybe it was easier to talk with him in the car because I couldn't look at him when I had to focus on the road. Or maybe since I'd already flashed my underwear, there wasn't a need to have secrets. Or it could have been because when Nate said he felt he was a disappointment to his dad, it made me realize that even though I'm always down on people for judging others by their looks, it's exactly what I'd done with him. Whatever the reason, there was no topic off-limits while we drove around the island. We covered:

1. The fact that both of us have dated losers in the past, including a discussion of who dated the

biggest loser. Nate won due to a time the girl he dated at boarding school cheated on him with his guidance counselor. Eeew.

2. Our life goals. Mine, to be an artist. Nate's, to be a teacher. We shared the fact that our parents both thought these were insane ideas and acted like we'd told them we wanted to be circus performers.

3. Our favorite things. Me: chocolate, the smell of paint, naps in the sunshine, and movies. Nate: his mom's homemade bread, lifting weights, books, and being near the water.

The only awkward moment was when we pulled into the driveway. Nate had noticed it was almost five and we'd better get back, and then there was a sudden silence that highlighted the fact that we shared the same home.

After dinner Nate went up to his room to tackle his homework. I went back to my room and grabbed my books. I stopped outside Nate's room. I wanted to continue our discussion, but I wasn't sure what the rules were. We lived together, but did that make it okay to just knock on his door? Should I make an appointment? In the end I scribbled *in the library* on a piece of paper and slid it under his door.

The library was cold, but it wasn't too bad with a pile of blankets. Sure, the living room would have electric light, but it would also have Dick and my mom. I wasn't prepared to break my mom's heart and tell her that my brief and glorious cheerleading career was already over. The oil lamp on the table gave off a decent amount of light. I ran my fingers along the mantel, looking at the framed pictures. My eyes caught on one in particular. There was a stern-looking woman wearing the beaded dress I had found in the attic. She was holding the hands of a little boy. A baby Dick. His mom looked like she had the personality of a prison warden. Her eyes didn't have a touch of softness, and her dark hair was pulled back in a severe bun as if it were afraid to misbehave. She might have been holding his hand, but the distance between her and the kid-size Dick was massive. On one of the lower shelves was a stack of Scrabble games. Dick wasn't kidding when he said the family members were big fans of the game.

I lit some extra candles and pulled out my American history textbook. We were supposed to have a test tomorrow. I'd missed the review this afternoon, so I was going to have to figure out on my own what random thing Mr. Mills was going to focus on for the test. I managed to read two chapters before my brain was at risk of overload. There are only so many facts about the Great Depression a person can shove into their head before they become depressed themselves. I looked at my watch. It was almost eleven, but I didn't feel tired.

I pulled out my sketchpad. I let the pencil take the lead instead of trying to plan out a picture. I stopped when I realized what

I was drawing. A seashell. I'd sketched in nautilus shells leaning against each other with a single sand dollar in the foreground. I hadn't thought about the ghost stuff all day. Things had been going so well with Nate, it didn't seem like the time to ask him what he thought of the idea of his dead sister trying to send me a message. I used the side of the pencil to fill in the shadows. I wanted to give the impression that the shells were balanced on each other, resting, but not weighing each other down. I wasn't sure where all the details were coming from. I didn't consider myself to be an expert on any type of marine life, but if I paused for a beat, then my pencil would start to move. I held the sketch out to get a better look. That's when I heard my mom calling my name.

Her voice was raised, coming from the other wing of the house. I stepped into the hallway at the same time she flung open the heavy wooden door between the two wings. She was wearing her bathrobe and her hair was standing on end. She pointed a finger at me.

"There you are."

I took a step back. I could tell she was barely holding it together.

Dick rushed in on my mom's heels. "I shouldn't have said anything. I never meant to upset you. I'm sure Isobel can explain." He patted her back. His face was pulled down into an exaggerated frown. I had a hunch that whatever he had said to my mom had been specifically designed to upset her.

"I'd like to hear her explain this." Mom held out her hand to show me something, but she was shaking and the objects fell. I looked down at the floor where they crashed, a pile of seashells.

My face scrunched up. "Where did you find these?"

"I found them right where you left them. They're all over the house." Her voice shook. "I'm worried about you, Isobel."

"I didn't do anything," I stammered.

"Now, we talked about this," Dick said to my mom. "You can't let yourself get upset. What Isobel's doing is a call for help. It's not in her control. What we need to do is let her know we hear that call and we're not going to ignore this or sweep it under the carpet."

I looked back and forth between them, trying to figure out what was going on. Mom's eyes glanced down and her nostrils flared in annoyance. She yanked the sketchbook out of my hands. The metal spiral caught the soft flesh between my thumb and forefinger, and an angry red slash of blood appeared.

"You didn't do anything? Then explain this." She thrust the sketchbook toward me so that the paper was an inch from my face.

Dick shook his head sadly as if instead of a picture it was a terminal medical diagnosis. "I was afraid of this."

"Afraid of what? I drew a picture. It's just a picture."

Nate came into the library, his eyes widening when he saw what was going on.

"There are seashells all over the house. Dick stepped on one at the top of the stairs. He could have slipped and hurt himself.

Now I find you drawing pictures of seashells. Either you did this and don't remember, or you're doing it and now lying about it." Mom's lower lip shook.

Dick pushed his facial expression into something that was supposed to resemble concern, but I could tell it was way closer to a feeling like enjoyment.

I didn't say anything. I couldn't explain, so it didn't seem that it would be a good idea to try.

Dick shook his head sadly at my mom. "We need to go ahead with what we discussed. I can't have you this worried."

"Of course not," my mom agreed, not meeting my eyes.

"What have you discussed?" I asked, looking back and forth between them.

"You need an evaluation," Dick said.

"Evaluation for what?" My voice raised an octave.

"You need to see someone."

"You're sending me to a shrink?" I glanced over to Nate, afraid to see what he must be thinking.

"There's no reason to become hysterical. With the way you've behaved, many people would have simply checked you into residential care. We're trying to find a middle ground, to make sure you get the help you need," Dick said.

"Residential? Do you mean a psych ward?" I yelled.

"The way you're acting now makes me think residential might be what you need." My mom dropped the sketchbook at my feet and ran out of the room.

"She's very upset. She's concerned for you. I'm concerned for you. When I saw these all over the house I knew it had to be you. This picture just confirms it. Your mom has tried to avoid reality where you're concerned, but I'm not going to allow that. Mental health problems run in your family. Your behavior is erratic. You don't like me for some reason and you feel the need to act out. I hope that's all it is. I checked around, and there's someone here on the island. You can head this off before your problems overwhelm you. And if we can't tackle this here, then we'll take it to the next level."

"What if I don't want to go?"

"That isn't an option," Dick said as he walked out of the room.

I bent down to pick up my sketchbook. I couldn't look at Nate.

"You okay?" he asked.

"I'm not crazy," I said softly.

Nate crossed the room and crouched down next to me so that we were face-to-face. He stared me straight in the eyes. "I believe you." He opened his arms and I fell into them.

Chapter 24

Nate slid open the library window and crawled out. He held out his hand, and I took it, following him into the night.

"The house alarm is only set for the doors. If we go out this way, no one will know," Nate said.

"I can explain about the mental health thing," I said.

"Don't worry about it. Let's just get out of here."

It was cold outside and I shivered. He pulled off his sweatshirt and gave it to me. I pulled it on, enjoying that it was still warm. We walked across the flagstone patio toward the garden. He slipped between two bushes, and we were on a trail I didn't know even existed. It wound downhill.

I tripped over something and Nate caught me before I could fall. "Careful, that's the old well cover."

"That's all I need to do is fall down a well." I stepped carefully around the wooden top.

"It hasn't been used for years. It used to be all rotted, but my dad capped it over years ago. You could dance the tango on that thing and not fall through."

"Where are we going?"

"Almost there."

Either Nate must have been down this path a thousand times before or he had bat sonar, because he didn't take a single misstep. I on the other hand seemed to trip on everything, including stray atoms. I was certain I was going to take a face-plant at any moment. There was a gap in the rocks ahead, and Nate turned so he could slide through. I said a mental prayer that my butt wouldn't wedge me in. I was so focused on not getting stuck that it took me a second to notice the view.

"Whoa." I didn't have the words to describe it better than that. We had wound our way down so that we were on the beach. The sand looked white in the moonlight, and trees that had washed up on the beach were lined up like hurdles. The waves came out of the darkness to ripple over the sand. It felt like we were standing at the edge of the world.

"Come down this way." Nate picked his way down to the beach, grabbing stray branches as he went, until we were at a pit framed by rocks. He tossed the wood into the pit and crouched down. "Can you stand over here? It will block the wind."

"Sure." I moved to stand next to him, and he reached into a

hole in the log next to us and pulled out a plastic bag that had a box of matches inside. He lit the wood and blew softly on it until it caught. Then he pulled me down so I was sitting next to him. We leaned against the log. The sound of the fire crackling mixed with the regular beat of the waves. It was strangely relaxing.

"My mom used to come down here to the beach with me and my sister all the time." He stretched his legs out so they were to the side of the fire. "I remember once when I was like ten, my mom woke up my sister and me in the middle of the night and brought us down here to see a meteor shower. It was the most amazing thing. She said it was angel fireworks."

"Does your dad come down here?"

"No. My mom was the one who loved this kind of thing. My dad isn't much of an outdoors fan." He shrugged and looked away.

"You okay?"

"I still can't believe she and my sister are gone. Right after it happened it felt like I was going to die. It didn't seem like anyone could hurt that much and still live. Now it's weird because there are blocks of time when life seems normal. I'll be reading a book or watching a TV show and not thinking about it at all, and then suddenly the fact that they're dead hits me and it's like it happened all over again for the first time."

I touched his arm. "I wish I knew what to say."

"There isn't anything anyone can say. My mom and I had a fight the day she died. I don't really remember what it was about, something stupid like leaving the milk out. Now I keep thinking if I had known it was going to be the last time I saw her, I wouldn't have been such a jerk. And my sister . . ." Nate raised his eyebrows. "She could drive you nuts in record time. She was always touching my stuff and breaking it. I can't even count the number of times I yelled at her."

"I bet she still knew you loved her. Your mom, too."

"Hope so. You remind me a bit of her."

"I bug you, so I remind you of your sister?"

Nate laughed. "I meant my mom. She did her own thing, didn't try and fit into anyone's set role for her. She would have liked you."

I blushed. I wasn't sure what to say. I ran my hands through the sand. A seashell was caught between my fingers. I turned it end over end, looking at it in the light of the fire. Nathaniel reached over and took it from my hands.

"My sister used to collect shells. She would stack them up into these piles. My mom called them fairy houses. My mom would tell us these long, complicated stories about the fairies who lived in them and how they would grant wishes for people who made the houses for them. After that Evie made them all the time. She was like a one-woman fairy condo queen. I remember my sister had one she kept on the side of her bed. One winter I found her stacking those mini-marshmallows next to it. She couldn't always explain what she was doing very well—her language skills were poor. She couldn't always come up with the right word to explain what she meant, but I had the feeling she was leaving them like gifts."

"The seashells in the house . . ." My voice trailed off. I wasn't sure how to ask the question.

"They were set up like her fairy houses. They were everywhere. On the stairs, in the kitchen, the hallway. There must have been dozens of them all over the house."

"I didn't put them there." I was sure I hadn't, almost 100 percent sure. I'd been studying history. I could tell you all about the New Deal, so I couldn't have been in some sort of fugue state littering the house with seashells. I thought about the sketch. That was a coincidence. I'd been thinking about shells since I'd had that dream. And it didn't matter how crazy a person was, there was no way drawing a picture of something in one room made that thing appear in another part of the house. I bit my lip.

"I know you didn't do it."

"Then who do you think did it?"

Nate shrugged.

"My friend Anita thinks your sister is trying to send a message."

Nate raised an eyebrow. "What is she trying to say?"

"She's your sister. Your guess is as good as mine."

"Nothing against your friend Anita, but I don't believe in ghosts." Nate shifted and rubbed his hands on his pants. "I don't think the shells got in the house from the other side."

"Your dad thinks I did it but don't remember doing it." I

waited to see if he would jump on the comment or ask more about my mental health.

Nate sighed. "I suspect my dad might have done it."

I sucked in a surprised breath. "Why?"

"My dad hates coming in second. He'd make a lousy supporting actor. If there's a spotlight, then he wants to be in it. He used to get annoyed when my mom would pay too much attention to either my sister or me."

The idea of Dick competing with his disabled daughter for his wife's attention struck me as pathetic. "So you think he did this so that my mom would be mad at me?"

"Sounds bad, doesn't it?" Nate chewed on his lower lip. "I'm not sure he set out with the idea of getting you in trouble, but he'd love her turning to him to be the savior, the big problem solver. He likes being hero-worshipped."

I wasn't sure what was worse, the idea of Nate's sister trying to send a message from beyond the grave or my stepdad manipulating my mom so he could come first with her. My mom and I had never been best friends, but we'd never been as on edge with each other as we'd been since we moved here. I looked up at the stars and gathered my courage. "You remember when I told you there was something embarrassing about my family, but then I wouldn't tell you what it was?" I thought he might say something flip, but he stayed serious.

"I remember. You don't have to tell me."

"No, I want to. Besides, you probably already guessed. The

thing is, my dad was sick. I mean, he is sick; it's just controlled now. He has schizophrenia."

"Okay." Nate threw another branch on the fire.

"That's it?"

"You were expecting me to run screaming into the night?"

"Maybe."

"Keep in mind you're talking to a guy who has quite a few interesting people in his family tree."

"Schizophrenia can be genetic."

"Doesn't mean you're destined to have it. Are you trying to convince me you're crazy?"

"No. I just thought you should know."

"Is your dad a good guy?"

"I guess. I don't see him much."

"Why not?"

"Things with him and my mom got pretty ugly when they split up. It wasn't that I took my mom's side, but I lived with her, and he left when I was really young. I'm not really sure which one of us stopped trying first, but we just sort of drifted apart."

"You ever think of getting in touch with him now?"

I pulled on a loose string at the end of my T-shirt. "You know, I haven't. Which, now that I say it, sounds really strange. Normal people would, wouldn't they?"

"I think you worry too much about being normal. Unique isn't a bad thing. You might want to get in touch. There's not much worse than wishing you had said something once it's too late to say anything." Nate touched my hand and an electric bolt shot up my arm. "I'm glad you told me."

"Me too."

"Of course, now that we know each other's deep, dark secrets, I guess we're stuck with each other."

"We are, huh?" My heart sped up. Was he saying what I thought he was saying? Could he actually like me? He trusted me with his vintage car. We'd been having all these meaningful conversations. He saved me from flashing my undies to the entire student body. He didn't think I was crazy, which I grant is not the same as liking me, but it certainly had to be pointing in the right direction. Then again, I'd thought I could pull off being a cheerleader, and how wrong was I about that? Then there was the fact that he was my stepbrother. What I was feeling wasn't technically illegal, but it still felt wrong. I really wished Anita and I were talking, because she would be way better at sorting out what was going on.

"I know I wasn't the greatest when you moved here."

"It's okay. It was a weird situation." I licked my lips in case he had any kissing urges and I got a mouthful of sand. "Pfffft." I spit. Great. Nothing more romantic than someone hacking gobs of saliva onto the ground.

"You okay?"

"Sand," I explained in case he thought I was just a random spitter.

"Here. You have some still on your lips." Nate leaned

toward me and ran his thumb across my mouth. I could feel a few course grains slide between my mouth and his thumb. His hand stayed cupping my chin, and I looked up. His eyes locked onto mine and he pulled me closer. I felt my breath quicken. His mouth was warm, and when his lips touched mine, it felt like every bone in my body went soft. I just melted into his arms. Nate was strong, and he lifted me so that I nestled in his lap. He smelled like the campfire. His chin rubbed like sandpaper on my face, but it didn't bother me in the least.

I'd made out with plenty of guys before, but it was never like this. Usually it was awkward, with an elbow getting stuck in between, or an awareness that I was wearing my nasty, slightly gray sports bra, or sometimes there seemed to be too much spit, so that the whole thing felt like there was a rabid garden slug in my mouth, or the guy would grope my chest like he was testing cantaloupes for their ripeness factor. This was completely different. It was like puzzle pieces clicking together. We fit. I felt like we couldn't get close enough. I pulled back long enough to yank his sweatshirt over my head. I was plenty warm enough without it. Nate made a soft sound and began to kiss the arch of my neck, his hands wound into my hair as if he planned to consume me right there on the beach.

I don't know how far things would have gone, but a sudden crack of lightning made us both look up. The sound of thunder rolled across the water an instant before the rain started to fall.

"We'd better get back," Nate said. He stood and pulled me up after him. He kicked sand onto the fire while grabbing the sweatshirt I had tossed to the side. The rain started to fall faster.

"This changes things, doesn't it?" I asked tentatively.

Nate stopped trying to make sure the fire was out and took me by the hand. He pulled me closer and kissed me again. Our wet clothes stuck to our skin.

"I hope so. I wouldn't want to go back."

Chapter 25

When I got to school the next morning there was a giant pair of panties duct taped to my locker. They were designed for someone roughly the size of a Volkswagen. I peeled them off with a loud ripping sound. My locker was sticky from the tape residue. If a small freshman leaned against it, he'd be stuck there like it was a giant piece of flypaper. This was exactly the kind of thing that would have upset me a day ago. Post–Nate kissing, the situation seemed juvenile. He'd driven me to school this morning, and we parked in the back row where we engaged in some pre-school making out. He was better than a double espresso; I was practically humming with energy. We'd decided to play things cool at school. Everyone didn't need to know our business. There was plenty for people to be talking about already.

"Where were you yesterday?" Sam asked, coming up behind me.

"I left." I handed Sam the fat panties and started to fish through my locker to find my copy of *The Crucible* for English class. Sam realized what she was holding and dropped them on the floor. I kicked them in the general direction of the trash can.

"Eww. Whose panties are those?" Sam wiped her hand on her sweater.

"No idea."

"I should warn you, Nicole's a bit ticked," Sam said, shifting her books to her other hip.

"She's ticked at me?"

"Even though you're an alternate, you were still supposed to go down to the ferry terminal to see the team off."

I slammed my locker door and looked at Sam. "Are you kidding me? Did she honestly expect me to be standing down there like nothing happened?"

Sam shrugged like the whole conversation was entirely too complicated for her. It was a really good thing Sam was pretty, because she did not have "college bound" written all over her.

"I'm quitting cheerleading," I said.

Sam's mouth dropped open like I had confessed to sleeping with Principal Hoffman. "You can't quit."

"I already did." I'd dropped off my uniform, or at least the few parts of it I was provided, at Ms. Lancaster's room that morning. "Let's be honest, Sam, cheering was never really my thing."

"Nicole's going to freak."

"Why? What does it matter to her?" I started walking toward class. Sam followed behind me.

"She's sort of used to people doing what she wants."

"Well, it's a brand-new day."

Sam grabbed my arm to make me slow down. "Nicole isn't the kind of person you want to have ticked at you."

"What are you trying to say? Should I watch my back?"

Sam chewed her bottom lip. "I'm not trying to sound dramatic. It's just that Nicole can be kinda harsh. Like once, there was a girl that used to go to school here who kissed Nicole's ex-boyfriend. Only, Nicole was really mad because she and this guy had only broken up a few days before, and Nicole thought she was being a total bitch for moving in so fast."

"So what happened? Did Nicole do away with her and bury her under the football field by the light of the full moon?"

"I'm not joking. Nicole made her life miserable. Debra couldn't take it. Then, because people wanted to get on Nicole's good side, they all joined in. Debra was crying all the time, and then her parents decided to homeschool her." Sam whispered the last part like we were CIA spies exchanging information in hostile territory.

"If there is anyone who has a right to be mad, it's me. Nicole left me up there shaking what my mother gave me in a pair of polka-dot underwear. She can say it was a joke, but I'm smart enough to know when the joke is on me. If I can forgive, forget, and move on, then so can she. I'm dropping cheering. If that means Nicole doesn't want to be my friend anymore, then that's fine. If I'm really honest, I'm not even sure it would be any big loss. She might be the biggest thing going on this island, but there is life off this island. I'm not scared of her."

I started walking again. I didn't want to be late for class. I'd sounded confident when I talked to Sam, but when I saw Nicole leaning outside the doorway of my first class, I stopped suddenly. Sam ran into me, nearly knocking me to the floor. Nicole was smiling, but it didn't reach her eyes. Her eyes had more of that Charles Manson look to them. Sam took one look at her and mumbled something about being late and took off in the other direction.

"I stopped by Ms. Lancaster's room this morning and she said you quit the squad." Nicole's voice had the "I'm very disappointed in your behavior" parent tone to it.

"Yep." I held my books in front of my chest like a shield.

"You're not going to quit over a silly joke, are you?"

"No."

Nicole's smile grew wider.

"I'm quitting because I never should have let you talk me into joining."

Nicole's smile froze in place. "I put myself out to get you on the squad. Do you know how many girls in this school would kill for a chance to be a part of the team?"

"Great. Then you won't have a problem filling the spot." I

moved past Nicole and into the room. I plunked down in my desk and let myself take a deep breath.

"Hey, Izzy," Nicole called out from the hallway. "We'll finish this conversation later, okay?" She didn't wait for me to say anything before walking away.

Chapter 26

There was no escaping going to the psychologist/shrink/ skull jockey. My mom insisted on driving me to the appointment. I kept telling myself that, other than wasting my time, there was no reason not to see a shrink, but I couldn't shake the feeling he would take one look at me and declare me officially crazy.

"Dr. Mike comes very highly recommended." This was at least the one billionth time my mom had pointed this out. I think she wanted to assure me that even though she was forcing me to see a shrink, at least she'd picked a good one. Neither of us mentioned that Dr. Mike was the only one on the island.

"Why does he call himself Dr. Mike? Who does he think he is? Cher? Madonna? Dr. Phil?"

"I think he prefers the approachability of having patients call him by his first name."

"Maybe he doesn't want us to have his last name in case we start stalking him."

Mom pulled up to a house. It was a Victorian house painted a light purple. The gables and arches were painted yellow and red. Clearly, Dr. Mike was not afraid of color.

"Is this his *house*?"

"His office is there on the side," my mom said, pointing to a small sign outside.

"His business can't be doing very good if he has to work out of his home. Plus this totally blows his first-name-only antistalking plan."

"Don't start, Isobel." My mom unbuckled her seat belt and opened her door. I grabbed her arm before she could get out.

"I don't need you to come in with me. I can do this by myself." It seemed to be a bad plan to have her there talking about my family history and recent tendency to have nightmares. I preferred to pace the rate of information Dr. Mike was going to get.

"All right. Call me if you want a ride home."

"It's okay, I'm going to the library after this." I opened my door and climbed out. I was just about to shut the door when my mom called out again.

"I'm sorry this move has been so hard for you." Her hands were clenched on the steering wheel, and she wouldn't look me in the face.

I shrugged. "It's okay. I'm getting used to things."

"Things with Richard just happened out of the blue, and then he wanted to marry right away. He wouldn't even imagine living anywhere else. I was afraid . . ." Her voice trailed off. "It sounds pathetic, doesn't it? I was afraid if I didn't say yes right there and then that he might just disappear. I would have missed my chance."

I felt myself flush in embarrassment for her. "Nah. He was the one who was lucky to get a chance with you."

She gave me a small smile. "Maybe. I hope you know, I never would have done anything if I thought it would make you sick." She picked at her thumbnail.

If she hadn't been in the car, I would have hugged her. "I know, Mom. It's okay. I'm okay."

She took a deep breath and seemed to pull herself together. "I want you to know I'm proud of you for coming. We can't tackle what we won't face."

I shut the door. She and Dick hadn't even been married two months and she was already starting to sound like him. I watched her drive away before slowly climbing the steps to the office. I'd convinced her I was okay. Now I just had to convince a professional.

Dr. Mike opened the door and smiled, offering me his hand to shake. "You must be Isobel."

"That's one of my personalities," I said amiably. "You can meet the other twelve once we get started." He got credit for not freaking out at my lame attempt at humor. His lips sort of tensed a bit, but that was it. He stepped aside so I could walk into his office.

His office had once been a porch. He had added walls and winterized it, but you could still tell. The office ran the length of the house, with one wall being floor-to-ceiling bookcases. There were a couple of comfortable-looking chairs and his desk.

"Where's the couch?" I asked, looking around.

"No couch."

"Where am I supposed to lie down and tell you all about my childhood?"

"This isn't psychotherapy."

"Oh." I wandered along the bookshelves. You can tell a lot about a person by what kinds of books and things he keeps around. There was a whole shelf of signed baseballs imprisoned in clear Lucite boxes. I picked one up and looked inside. I couldn't make out whose signature it was. "You must like baseball, huh?"

"I do. How about you? Mariners fan?"

"Not really. All that running around in circles. Seems sort of pointless." I looked over, hoping I hadn't offended him. This was the guy who could get me locked up. "Not that there's anything wrong with baseball. National pastime and all."

My finger ran down the shelf. Then I saw it. I picked up the picture frame and held it close to my face so I could be sure. No doubt about it. I turned around to face him and held out the frame.

"You must know Nicole. You look about her age. She's my daughter," he said.

Oh no. What were the odds that my new shrink would have spawned Nicole? Add this to the list of reasons why I hate living in a small town. If I had to see a shrink in Seattle, there would have been buckets to choose from, and none of them would be related to anyone I knew.

"Let me assure you, everything you say here is confidential."

"Yeah. I'm sure." I moved closer to the door. I could picture the entire Percy family sitting down to a wholesome meal of meatloaf and mashed potatoes with a bowl of lumpy gravy and Dr. Mike saying, *"You'll never guess who was in the office today."* The last thing I needed was for Nicole to have a big, juicy secret of mine.

"I'm afraid there isn't another counselor on the island. If you don't feel comfortable, I can make a referral for someone on the mainland."

Shit. I was stuck. I suspected Dick would skip the hassle of having to ferry me back and forth to talk to someone and instead convince my mom to toss me into a mental ward where I could stay out of his hair and he'd have her all to himself. I imagined myself wearing institutional pajamas and having to eat everything with a spoon because no one would trust me with a fork or knife. Most likely my roommate would be some freakish, giant-size woman who didn't speak because she'd chewed off her own tongue.

"We might be able to make this work as long as you mean it about keeping things just between us." I stuffed my hands in my pockets. "So what do we do?"

"Let's start by sitting down." Mike motioned to the chairs.

I plunked down next to him and pulled my sleeves over my hands. "I was joking about the multiple personality thing. You knew that, right?"

"I was pretty sure. Why don't you tell me about what brings you here?"

"I'm guessing my mom already told you the whole story."

"She mentioned a few things, but I'd rather hear it from you."

I took a deep breath. "I guess it starts with my dad."

I told Dr. Mike everything. How my dad had been the very model of a fine outstanding citizen until he started having all these paranoid thoughts. His whole world exploded, and my mom and I got left behind. I told him that my mom blamed my dad for how her life turned out and how I suspected she thought my dad did it on purpose somehow. I told him my mom was worried I was going crazy just like my dad.

"What about you?"

"What about me?"

"Do you think you're going to inherit the same difficulties as your dad?"

"Of course I worry about it. It's not a difficulty; it's a huge thing."

"What if you did inherit your father's mental illness?"

"So you think I have it?" My heart seemed to lock in place.

"That's not what I said. I asked you to tell me what you think it would mean if you did. Sometimes it's best to deal with things straight on. Tell me what it would mean if you were diagnosed with a mental illness."

"It would mean my life is over."

"Is your father's life over?"

"No." I slouched down in the seat, feeling grumpy for some reason.

"You told me your dad is reasonably successful as an artist. His condition is well managed and has been"—he looked down at his notes—"for at least thirteen years now. He has friends, I assume? A social life."

"He's not a hermit or anything."

Dr. Mike didn't say anything. He just looked at me with this annoying smile on his face. I looked out the window, trying to wait him out, but the guy was a professional. I buckled and broke the silence.

"Okay, my dad is doing all right, but you can't possibly think that being crazy is a good thing."

"I'm not trying to say that having a mental illness would be preferred, but I'm asking you to explore your statement about it being the end of your life."

I leaned my head back so I was looking at the ceiling. "This conversation hurts my brain."

"Then we're making progress," Dr. Mike said, sounding way

too perky about it. "You say your mom is worried that you're developing a mental illness, but what I want to tackle is if you are worried about it."

I shrugged, my shoulders feeling tight. I swallowed to keep from bursting into tears. That was the issue. It didn't matter what Dick or my mom thought. What really freaked me out was the idea that I thought I might be crazy.

"You don't need to answer. We'll take some small steps together. I'd like to encourage you to reach out to your dad as a place to start. You could write him a letter or give him a call. It would be good for you to talk."

"About what?"

"That's up to you."

"I don't really have anything to say to him."

"Maybe it's time you did. Ask him about his experiences, ask him how his life is going, how he copes with managing his illness. Now, let's get down to your homework for our next meeting."

"There's homework?" I sat up straight. "I'm already under a lot of pressure at school. Are you sure you should be putting more on my shoulders? I could snap. I have to think that wouldn't look good for you. Could you live with the guilt?"

"I'll do the best I can. Don't worry, this homework doesn't require you to write a paper. One of the things I heard you say when you talked about your own health is that you feel out of control."

"Well, yeah. How does someone beat genetics? It's like

wishing you had control over blue eyes. If I have this condition, there's nothing I can do."

"Research tells us that people who feel a sense of control over their lives express greater levels of happiness. I want you to identify an aspect of your life that currently feels like it is happening *to* you and turn it around so you're in control. You've been dealing with a lot of changes recently; it'll be good for you to tackle one of them and be in control of it."

"Like what?"

"That's up to you."

I rubbed my forehead. "Can't you just give me a test or something and tell me if I'm crazy? Maybe have me look at an inkblot and tell you what I see."

"I'm afraid it isn't that easy. I'm not going to make any snap judgments, and neither are you. We're going to talk and discover things together. You're not alone in this, Isobel."

"Of course not, I've got all those other multiple personalities to keep me company." I stared at him across the desk; he didn't crack a smile. "That was a joke," I clarified.

He smiled and made a note in my file.

Chapter 27

I kicked the leaves on the sidewalk as I walked to the library. I wondered if there would be any way I could get some time alone with Nate later. I wanted to talk with him about Dr. Mike's plan for me to contact my dad.

I couldn't recall a time when my dad and I were close. I had some memories: him taking me to see Santa Claus at the mall and him wearing my mom's frilly apron to make his specialty lasagna. The thing is, I wasn't even sure whether they were my own memories or stories other people told that I'd hijacked to fill in my past. My parents split up when I was four, and from what my mom told me, he was pretty sick for a few years.

One memory I knew was mine was first-grade parents' day at school. I remember that my mom made me wear a dress and it had a lace collar that itched. I was nearly bouncing in my seat waiting for Miss Klee to finish her welcome speech so I could talk to my mom. It seemed very exciting to have her there at school. All the grown-ups were standing at the back of the room, and I easily picked my mom out. Most of the other moms were in jeans or khakis. My mom was wearing a pink suit with matching pink shoes. She'd had to take the afternoon off from her job at the law firm. I couldn't wait to show her the picture I had made in art class. It was the best of the whole group. I could tell Miss Klee thought so too, because she had placed it right in the middle of the wall.

There was a shuffle at the back, and I heard my mom raise her voice. I cringed. I didn't know what I had done to get in trouble, and so much trouble that she would interrupt Miss Klee. Then I saw him. My dad had shown up. He was wearing a denim shirt that was splattered with paint. My mom was yelling at him to get out, that he had no right to be there. Miss Klee was flustered and trying to get control of her classroom back.

My dad crossed the room without answering my mom. He looked at the pictures on the back wall and picked mine out instantly.

"Is this one yours, pumpkin?" he asked, bending down at the side of my seat so we were on the same level.

I nodded.

"I knew it must be. Best one in the group." I remember my chest filling up with pride. My dad drew better than anyone I knew, and he thought my picture was good.

My mom came up and hissed in my dad's ear. All the other parents were looking at us. "Even she doesn't want you here. Can't you see you're embarrassing her?"

My dad and mom both looked at me.

"Do you want me to go?" my dad asked.

I looked at him and then at Mom. I could see she was angry, and I knew exactly what she wanted me to say; she wanted me to send him away. I liked that my dad had come, but I didn't see him that often. My mom I saw every day. When she was mad, no one was happy. I nodded my head yes. My eyes dropped to my desk. Even at that age I knew I'd betrayed him.

"There you go. She doesn't want you. Now leave. You've done enough."

And just like that my dad left. He didn't argue anymore with my mom, and he didn't try to have any regular visitation. I've seen him maybe a few dozen times since then, and he sends me a birthday card every year. I memorized his address, but I never wrote back and I certainly never went to visit. I realized now how much it must have hurt his feelings for me to reject him that day at school, but give me a break. I was six. He was the grown-up. It seems that he could have, that he *should* have, tried harder.

"I thought that was you. What are you doing here?"

I looked up in surprise; I'd been lost in my own thoughts and hadn't gotten very far down the block. Nicole was standing in front of me.

"Uh. I was just taking a walk." My heart raced.

"And just happened to be right by my house?" She cocked her head to the side.

Shit. She knew I was seeing her shrink dad. It would take less than thirty seconds for this to spread all over school. Heck, she probably had already texted the entire student body with the update.

"I know why you're here." Nicole sat down on the curb and motioned for me to sit. I sank down next to her. "I feel bad too."

"You do?"

"Sure. I really did mean the whole thing to be joke, but I know it was way out of line. I should have realized how it would feel to you, especially being new and all. The whole panty thing was rude. I'd hate if we weren't friends. I'm guessing since you're here you must hate the idea of us not being friends, too." Nicole put her hand on my arm. "So can we put it behind us?"

"Sure." I shifted my weight on the cement curb and tried to avoid looking at her house in case she could somehow tell I had been inside. "I should tell you, I'm still not up for giving cheerleading another try. It isn't my thing."

"Fair enough. Lucky for you, your best friends are on the squad." She linked arms with me, and I had to fight the urge to move away from her. "We'll make sure you get invited to all the best parties. Oh! Which reminds me, have you heard about the bonfire?"

I thought of the fire Nate and I made on the beach, but

I knew that wasn't what she was talking about. "No, I haven't heard anything."

"There's going to be a huge party at the beach on Tara Cove this Thursday. Chuck Watlin's brother bought him a keg, so there will be tons of beer. You'll come, won't you?"

"Sure."

"And I need to ask you a favor, too." Nicole gave a sly smile. "I want you to bring your brother with you."

"Nate?"

Nicole laughed. "Do you have any other brothers? Of course Nathaniel. I figure this is my perfect chance. I'll ply him with a few drinks and make my move."

My brain stuttered, trying to think of the right thing to say. "Nathaniel isn't big on parties. He's more of the quiet type."

Nicole brushed away my words like they were mosquitoes. "Everyone likes a party. It depends on the company. If he doesn't like crowds, he and I can slip away, just the two of us. All I'm asking is that you get him there."

"I'm not really comfortable with setting up Nate." I left off the bit where part of my discomfort came from the fact that I was dating him myself.

"It's not a fix-up. All I'm asking you to do is invite him. I'll do the rest." Nicole gave me a sidelong glance. "Certainly an invitation isn't asking too much." She laughed again. "If you keep this up, I'll think you want him for yourself."

I tried to join her laugh, but mine sounded hollow and empty.

"Perfect. Then it's settled." Nicole smiled and gave my knee a pat.

"I have to go. I need to get to the library before they close." I hated the feeling that I was asking her permission to leave.

"Of course." Nicole and I both stood. "Remember, I'm counting on you."

I waved to her as I walked away and hoped she would take that as an answer.

Chapter 28

The library was empty of other patrons. I smiled at the cranky librarian who was shelving books in the kid's section and dumped all my stuff on a table near the back. I pulled out a sheet of paper from one of my notebooks. I stared down at the blank page. You would think I'd have a lot of things to say to my dad since we hadn't talked in years, but I couldn't think of how to start. I chewed on the end of my pen for a bit before I tried to begin.

Dear Dad,

Surprise! It's me. I hope you're in the same place, because this is the only address I have for you. In case you haven't heard, we've moved. Mom got remarried and we're living on one of the islands now.

I saw some of your paintings in a gallery a couple of years ago. They were awesome. I should have told you then, but I didn't. I'm still drawing, but Mom's not crazy about it. I'm thinking about art school, but not sure.

There are actually a lot of things I'm not sure about. Nothing against Mom, but I thought it might be nice to have a different perspective on things once in a while. I'd like to be able to call you, if it's okay. If it's not, I understand. I'm seeing a shrink. Mom thought I should get some help getting my life on track. I can't really tell if I'm off track or not. Did you know?

I hope you're still painting and that life is good.

Your daughter,
Isobel

I read the letter over. It was lame. It was worse than lame. I felt like pounding my head on the table.

"Trouble thinking of what you want to say?" Mandy asked, leaning against the shelf at the end of the row.

I sighed. "It's a letter to my dad. We've been sort of estranged." I held up the paper. "I guess I thought sending a strange letter would fix things."

"Seems like a good place to start," Mandy said.

I liked that she didn't start fishing for details of why we were estranged or start offering advice about how when she was a kid she never got along with her parents either, and now she realized how they always had her best interests at heart. "I'm not sure where to begin," I said.

"Sometimes, how we say something doesn't matter as much as saying it in the first place," she said.

"Do you think I should send it?"

"There are envelopes and stamps in the top drawer of the desk." She nodded toward the check-out counter. "Take what you need. My treat." She smiled.

She was right. If I didn't send it now, I would lose my nerve. I marched up to the desk and pulled out an envelope. I wrote Dad's address down and practically slapped the stamp on. The older librarian came around the corner and stared at me behind the counter.

"I have permission. She said I could use one of the stamps." I pointed to Mandy. The older librarian followed my finger and then looked back at me.

"Oh." Her voice was flat.

I waved to Mandy before heading out the door. Now that I'd written the letter, I wanted to go home and see Nate and tell him about Nicole.

Downsides to living in the same house as the guy you like:

1. The chances of running into him in the hallway
    with seriously bad bed-head and morning breath

that smells like a week-old corpse left in the hot sun are high.

2. If you walk past his door at night, you'll discover he snores. That or he's keeping a running sawmill in there with competing chainsaws.

3. You can't watch your favorite cheesy TV shows without him knowing you have no taste. This leaves you pretending to have a huge interest in the stuff they show on public television.

4. He sees your weird eating habits, like how you like strawberry Pop-Tarts with peanut butter smeared on top.

5. Your favorite flannel pj's with the sock monkey design all over them have a seriously saggy ass, and thus you have to get up extra early so that you are dressed by the time you go downstairs for breakfast.

The major upside of living in the same place is that you see way more of him. Except, of course, when you really need to. I couldn't wait to talk to Nate and tell him about everything: seeing Dr. Mike, what happened with Nicole, and the letter to my dad. I flung open the front door and ran smack into Dick.

"Jesus!" I yelled out. Had he just been freaking standing there next to a closed door? Who the hell does that?

"Please don't cuss in this house," Dick said. "It isn't ladylike."

I did my best to avoid rolling my eyes. "Sorry," I mumbled. "Is Nate home?"

"Why?"

"Because I wanted to talk with him."

"What did your therapist say?"

Clearly, Dick wasn't going to let me find Nathaniel until we played twenty questions. "It's sort of private. Doctor-patient confidentiality and all that." If Dick thought I was going to let him have a peek into my brain, he was more deluded than the average schizophrenic. My mom stood in the doorway to the kitchen clutching a dish towel.

"I think Isobel's seeing Dr. Mike is a good step forward. Nip any problems right in the bud," my mom said.

"How in the world are we supposed to trust the medical opinion of someone who calls himself Dr. Mike?" Dick argued.

Even though I had mocked Dr. Mike's name, it was totally different when Dick did it.

"He has great credentials," my mom said, twisting the towel in her hands.

"Well, I hope so. It isn't that I want to cause trouble, but I also don't think we can afford to bury our heads in the sand. All I can say is that if we don't see some radical changes around here, we're going to need to look at other options."

"What are you talking about?" I asked.

"I think you need far more help than 'Dr. Mike' can give you. I spoke to someone in Olympia. He recommended that with your family history and current acting out, you would benefit from a residential program. At the very least until they get you on a working medication regime."

I felt my nostrils flare in annoyance. "I don't need medications." I turned to face my mom. "I don't need to be on drugs. There isn't anything wrong with me."

"Nothing wrong?" Dick shook his head sadly. "What would you call your behavior lately?"

"For the record, Dick," I put the emphasis on his name, "you're not my dad. So while I appreciate your input, decisions about my life aren't up to you."

"What goes on in this house is up to me," Dick fired back.

"What, you're planning to kick me out unless I do what you want? Do you think that's a threat? That sounds like a dream come true. Go ahead, tell me to leave. I can be on the next ferry back to Seattle. I have friends I can stay with so that I'm not cluttering up your house—oh, excuse me, I meant your estate." My face was inches from Dick's. I really hoped that if he called my bluff, Anita would forgive me for our fight. Otherwise it was going to be really awkward when I showed up at her place with my duffel bag and all my worldly belongings.

"Both of you stop it." Dick and I stopped our staring contest to look over at my mom. She was on the verge of tears and her lower lip was shaking. "We're a family now, and we solve problems as a family. No one is going anywhere." Mom shoved the towel under her arm and dashed past us up the stairs.

"I hope you're happy. You've upset your mother."

"*I've* upset her?" I snorted. I couldn't believe the arrogance of this guy. I shook my head. There was no point in arguing with him. "Excuse me, I need to speak to Nate." I stepped around Dick and headed for the stairs.

"Nathaniel's not home."

"Fine, I'll wait."

Dick grabbed my arm, his fingers digging into the flesh above my elbow. He pulled me close, and I could feel the spray of spit from his mouth when he spoke. "You stay away from him. I know your type." He looked me up and down like I was naked and he didn't like what he saw. "You think you can make yourself better by clinging to someone like Nathaniel. You need him for your reputation, and you're nowhere near good enough for him."

I yanked my arm back. "I have no idea what you're talking about." My heart was beating fast. Dick's "I'm a caring stepdad with your best interests at heart" act was officially over.

"Don't act like you don't know what I'm talking about. You need him to make yourself look good."

"I'm going to tell my mom what you said."

Dick laughed. "You do that. You turn to your mother like

a security blanket. You think she's going to believe you given everything going on?"

"I know what you're doing." I tried to keep my voice unwavering. "You're trying to convince my mom I'm crazy."

"It's not that hard of an argument to make."

"I'm not crazy."

Dick smiled. "I don't really care one way or the other."

I pushed past Dick and ran up the stairs to my room. I slammed the door loud enough so that it echoed through the whole house.

Chapter 29

Adults love to tell teens how this is the best time of our lives. How we should consider ourselves lucky to be living this "worry free" lifestyle. I can't tell if they say this stuff because they are completely delusional or they've forgotten what it is really like to be a teenager, or if they know how much it can suck, but they enjoy lying to us.

As a teen, you might not have the worries of a full-time job and having to pay a mortgage, but you do have to deal with the fact that you are completely at your parents' mercy. Your parents can decide (without any input from you) where you live, where you go to school. They can control what you wear. They tell you when you have to be home and try to decide who you're allowed to hang out with. They police what's on TV or if your house even has a TV. They decide when dinner is served and what you'll be eating. If they decide they want to be vegetarians, you're stuck trying to eat hot dogs on the sly.

Here's the real kicker: until you are eighteen, the law totally supports this domination. I knew a girl in my old high school. Her parents found religion and decided that she dressed too slutty. They cut up everything she owned. Including a pair of amazing expensive jeans that she had saved up her after-school job money to buy. Do you have any idea how many Happy Meals a girl has to make to buy designer jeans? A lot. They bought her a bunch of clothing that looked like it belonged on an eighty-year-old Amish woman. This girl went to the police because she figured there had to be some sort of law against your parents ruining your life, and she found out there was nothing she could do. Unless they're beating or molesting you, the authorities stay out of it. In fact, if you complain too much, you're considered a troublemaker. Your parents can force you to go to one of those teen boot camps where you have to sleep outside and eat cockroaches in order to learn some sort of valuable lesson.

Best time of our lives? Not freaking likely.

I sat folded up in the window seat in my room with Mr. Stripes the stuffed zebra in my lap. I hadn't bothered going down for dinner. There didn't seem to be any point in acting like everything was fine while Dick did his best to convince my mom to send me away. I kept waiting for Nate to come home, but it was getting dark and there was still no sign of him. After what Dick had said, I couldn't ask him where Nate was, so I was stuck waiting. He never carried his phone, so I couldn't call him. For all I knew he had moved out. While I waited, I kept thinking about what Dr. Mike said about taking control of some part of my life. I couldn't take control of Dick, as much as I would like to force him to bend to my will. I couldn't convince my mom that Dick was twisting everything I said and did. I couldn't control when Nate came home, because if long-distance mind control worked, he would have been here hours ago. If I could control where I lived, I would be on the next ferry so fast, all people would see is a blur as I ran down to the dock. Sure, I could take control of my health by exercising more, but I had the sense that wasn't going to make me feel better. I looked around the room. My eyes snagged on the pile of seashells that were still on my dresser. I walked over and picked one up. I tossed the shell into the air and caught it while I thought about it.

This was something I could tackle. I might as well take the lead. There were really only three options. Either Evie was intent on trying to send me a message, Dick was behind everything to get rid of me, or I was crazy. If neither of the first two options checked out, then I would have to go back to Dr. Mike and figure out what to do. My dad had done it. I could do it. I heard the crunch of gravel outside. I ran to the window and looked out just in time to see Nate pull his car into the drive. I yanked on a sweatshirt and grabbed my shoes and slipped down the stairs as fast as I could without making a sound. I paused in the foyer and listened. I could hear the murmur of the TV mixing with the voices of my mom and Dick talking.

The front door opened. Nate stopped short when he saw me. His mouth widened into a smile.

"Hey."

I pressed my fingers to his mouth and looked over my shoulder. The sounds from the family room didn't change. He took a step back and started to open his mouth again. I shook my head and slipped past him. I took a few steps and then motioned for him to follow me.

We walked down the driveway, staying close to the tree line in case anyone looked out the windows.

"Can you tell me what we're doing?" Nate whispered.

"I don't want our parents to overhear us." We rounded the corner to the orchard, and I stopped. The moonlight was brighter here.

"Come here." Nate pulled himself up into the nearest tree and perched on one of the branches.

I stood next to the tree and looked up at him. "Do you honestly think I can get myself up there? Do I look like Tarzan?"

"I keep forgetting you're from the city and never learned valuable survival skills like tree climbing." He hung on to the trunk with one arm and leaned over. "Give me your hand."

I reached up and he grabbed my arm and carefully pulled me into the tree. My legs spun like they were running up the trunk. The last guy I went out with, Josh, had been more of the creative type. He played guitar and wrote poetry. He and I used to make fun of jocks, but I had to say there was something very nice about a guy who had some muscles. Something very nice indeed. I had to fight the urge to ask Nate to do it again, or bench-press a pear tree for me.

We each sat on one of the thick branches. I held on to the trunk with one arm to avoid falling. Apparently, in addition to muscles, Nate had an inner squirrel. He didn't have any trouble balancing in the tree, whereas I felt like I could fall out anytime.

"Your dad and I had a huge fight. I don't think he likes me."

"Welcome to the club. I would tell you it's exclusive except the list of people my dad doesn't like is long. He hasn't liked me for years. If we had a few years, I'd tell you all the things I've done to disappoint him."

"You dad does like you. In fact, he wants to protect you from me. He told me to not bother trying to get my claws into you and drag you down to my level."

Nate laughed. "Bother. Definitely bother. I like the idea of you getting your claws into me."

"You know who else wants to get her claws in you?"

"You mean other than you? Am I going to have to install one of those take a number machines for all the women chasing me?"

I shoved him and nearly fell out of the tree from the effort. He laughed and grabbed me to make sure I didn't fall. I gripped the trunk harder. "Have you heard about the party coming up at Tara Cove?"

"Yeah."

"Nicole wants me to make sure you go. She's planning to make her move."

"Then I won't go. It's not really my kind of scene anyway."

"Sooner or later it's going to be an issue." I picked at the bark on the trunk. "Are we going to keep this hidden all year?" I hoped he wouldn't ask me what I meant by "this." I wasn't sure how to define our relationship, but I was sure that any definition I came up with wouldn't include Nicole slobbering all over him.

"What do you want to do?"

"Our parents will freak if it comes out that we . . . you know . . ." I was glad it was dark so he couldn't see how much I was blushing.

"You mean if it comes out that we like each other?"

I shrugged. Nate put his finger under my chin and tilted my face so that I was looking at him. "I don't care who it bothers. The only reason to hide it now is to keep people from trying to separate us."

We leaned toward each other. There was enough space separating us that I wasn't sure we could stretch without falling. I closed my eyes and felt his breath on my face an instant before his lips brushed mine. His mouth was warm. He pulled back and flashed me a half smile that made me want to yank my shirt off. Who knew a smile could be so sexy? He should be forced to have a permit for that smile.

"Did you bring me out here to make out in the trees or to tell me to watch out for Nicole?"

"Neither, but the making out part has been nice."

"Nice? That was my A game."

"Don't get me wrong, it wasn't bad." It was amazing, but I didn't say that. "If you need to practice, I'm willing to make some time for you."

"You're so selfless."

"A girl with a heart, that's how they describe me."

"I bet people have some very interesting ways to describe you." He leaned forward to kiss me again.

I put a hand up. If there was any more kissing, I was going to forget what I wanted to ask him. "I did bring you out to talk about something. I need your help."

"Sure."

"You might want to hear what it is first." I pulled on my lower lip. "I have sort of a project thing I need to do."

"For school?"

"No. It's more personal. I want to see if I can figure out what's going on around here, the strange stuff."

Nate pulled back. "I don't know if it's a good idea."

"Why?"

Nate jumped out of the tree, laced his fingers behind his head, and walked a few steps away. I leaned over. It seemed a long way to jump. I rolled over so that the branch was pressed into my stomach and then slid down until I was hanging by my hands before dropping to the ground. I landed on a rotting apple. It gave a soft squish under my foot. I scraped my shoe on the ground and then stood behind Nate, waiting for him to say something.

"You don't know what you're messing with. Maybe some things are best left alone."

"What if they're not? What if there is stuff we shouldn't be ignoring?" I looked him in the eye. "Do you think the whole thing is in my mind?"

"No, but that's not the same as believing this is all real, either. Maybe there's a ghost, or maybe the stuff you're seeing is just your mind making sense of information."

I felt a flare of annoyance. "My mind making sense of things? That sounds like you do think it is in my head."

"All I'm saying is sometimes our mind has a way of twisting things." Nate held up a hand to stop me from talking. "It's just as possible—heck, more possible—that a lot of this is stuff my dad has done to make sure he's got your mom's undivided attention."

"But that's the whole point. I shouldn't be sitting back and waiting to see what happens next. What I want to do is take back control, figure out what is going on. If it's your dad, I need to protect myself, and if your sister is trying to get a message to us, shouldn't we pay attention?"

Nate turned to face me. "Maybe some things are better left unknown."

Chapter 30

In the end, Nate reluctantly agreed to help me. I understood his hesitance. It wasn't that I wanted to muck about with possible ghosts. I am generally in favor of segregation of the dead and the living. However, I was in a situation where either I was crazy and doing these things without knowing it, my new stepdad was trying to make me look crazy, or there was a ghost. While I was willing to admit one of the defining characteristics of crazy people is that they don't know they're crazy, I couldn't accept that I had gone from sane to fully delusional in a matter of weeks. My mom always complains that I don't do anything fast, so why would this be any different? What I wasn't going to do was sit back and wait for Dick or Evelyn to make the next move. I was going to take Dr. Mike's suggestion and take control.

Nate offered to give me a ride, but I could tell he was less than thrilled to be seen in public asking the kinds of questions I wanted to ask, so I told him to wait at home and I'd ride my bike. Personally, I felt pretty safe. Librarians are like priests. You can tell them you want information on just about any subject and they never look at you weird. It's like a rule or something. I figured even in a small town like this, my question wouldn't be the strangest one the librarian had heard. I didn't know if librarians had any sort of official privacy code, but I was counting on confidence. They're not big talkers. It comes from being forced to be quiet all the time. Besides, I was starting to trust Mandy. I wouldn't go as far as to say we were friends, but I didn't have many people on this island I felt comfortable around.

I pulled open the door to the library. The older librarian was checking out books for a young mother who looked like she was about to lose it. The mother was holding a baby, had a stroller with what looked like twin girls around three, and had a five-year-old boy who was running around the shelves with his finger shoved up his nose. I considered warning him that if he fell, he would poke his brain out, but it struck me that losing intelligence was not something he was worried about. Either this woman had never heard of birth control or she was a masochist.

I didn't see Mandy anywhere, so I faked an interest in the New Books section while I waited. The heavy breeder was still getting organized, trying to get the books she'd taken out to fit into the shelf under the stroller. She would shove a book in, and then something, a juice cup, a Binky, or one disturbing Barbie-doll head, would fall out the other side. She would shove that back in, and then something else would leak out the other side. Her stroller was like a poorly designed clown car. I did my best to avoid sighing dramatically. This woman had enough problems.

I went over and helped. It was a good thing spatial relations were a strength of mine, because it required the geometry skills of Newton to get everything slotted into place. I even held the baby (who smelled like spoiled milk and stale Cheerios) so that the woman could corral the five-year-old, who was now in full meltdown mode. This kid had clearly never heard of the value of the inside voice.

By the time she left, I saw Mandy standing in the stacks. She was smiling. "Nice of you to help. Do you like kids?"

"Only with barbecue sauce."

At first I thought she was going to think I was serious, but then I saw the corners of her mouth twitch. Another bonus point in her favor—she got my sense of humor.

"So are you looking for cookbooks today?"

"No." My eyes slid away from her. I took a deep breath before I could lose my resolve and end up asking for a book on art history and running for the door. "I need some research materials."

"Another school project?"

"No, this one is a more personal interest."

"Go on."

I looked around the library to confirm the other librarian

wasn't listening in and no one else had come in. The last thing I needed was to discover someone like Nicole lurking behind a shelf. "I need some books on ghosts."

It was hard to tell, librarians being the bookish indoor type and not typically known for their dark tans, but it seemed like Mandy went pale.

"You mean ghost stories? Something like Poe or Stephen King?"

"No. I mean books about ghosts. How to find them, stuff like that."

"I see." Her fingers brushed nonexistent dust off the shelf closest to us. "You want something on the study of paranormal activity."

"Exactly."

She opened her mouth, and I waited for her to ask me the next question, but after a beat she closed it again and walked to the back corner of the library. I trailed after her. She began pointing at books as we went. *Real Life Haunting, Ghosts of the Pacific Northwest, Paranormal Investigator.* After she pointed out the first two, I realized that she never even bothered to look anything up on the computer. She was like a homing device for books. I wondered if she had a photographic memory of where every book could be found in the library or if this was a subject that enough people requested that she had no trouble finding it.

"Thanks." I sat at the closest table so I could look through the stack.

"Do you need anything else?"

I flipped through the top book and answered without even glancing up. "Nope. This is great." I turned a few more pages before I realized that she hadn't left. I looked up. She was still standing next to the shelf, watching me. Her eyebrows were scrunched together. I closed the book and met her eyes.

"Do you mind if I ask why you're interested?"

I paused. There really isn't a good way to tell a relative stranger that you think dead people are trying to tell you something. It's personal information. It's like telling someone you just met that you have a yeast infection. It might be true, but it's not the kind of thing people want to know about you. Plus, you know that every time they see you after that it will be the first thing they think about: *There she is, the girl with the yeast infection/ghost problem.* On the other hand, maybe she could help me. She was a librarian after all. They know all kinds of things.

"Lots of people think where I live, Morrigan, is haunted," I said.

"Have you seen anything?"

My eyes slid away from hers. "It's an old house. It's the kind of place where it's easy to freak yourself out." Talk about an understatement.

Mandy sat down at the table next to me. "I want to tell you something. I should have said something when you were here last time, but I sometimes forget people who haven't lived on the island their entire lives don't know all the details. It can be nice to meet someone who doesn't know everything about you." She gave me a half smile. "It lets people see you in a way others can't."

"I get that."

"When you looked through the historical records, do you remember the story about the girls who disappeared?"

"They said they were going out to Morrigan to look for ghosts." I wondered if I was about to get a lecture on how teens shouldn't mess around with things like paranormal activity.

Mandy took a deep breath. "I knew them."

Suddenly I felt guilty, as if I were the one who had done something to her friends. Like my connection to the house made me complicit in what happened. "I'm sorry," I mumbled.

Mandy leaned closer, and I sensed she wanted to give me a hug, but she pulled back. "It's okay. It's been a long time now. You remind me of one of them a little. Not the way you look, but your attitude. Both of you are too big for this island. Big dreams. Big plans."

"You don't think she just left the island, then?"

"No." Mandy brushed her hair out of her face. "She wanted to move off the island, but she never would have left without saying something. They made a big thing out of the fights she had with her parents, but those didn't mean anything. They were simply the fights kids have with their parents."

"I fight with my mom all the time."

"She wanted to be independent, but she loved her family.

Something happened to her." She met my eyes. "Something happened to those girls at that house."

I took a deep breath. "When I told you that the house was just old and kind of creepy, that wasn't the whole truth. I have seen things. Things have happened. The thing is, I don't know if it's supernatural or something someone is doing, trying to make me think it's supernatural." I looked down at the table. "Does that sound crazy?"

Mandy ran her hands over the stack of books on the table. "People read these in an effort to make sense of things. Make sense of things that have no explanation. But you know, I'm a bit of an unofficial expert on ghosts after what happened to me."

"Did you? Make sense of things, I mean?"

"Not yet, but I haven't given up trying."

I shivered. "The whole idea of ghosts seems weird."

"Not that weird. There was a time when people would think it was weird not to assume there was contact from those who had passed on. People used to be more comfortable with the idea of an afterlife and the interaction between the worlds of the living and dead. For example, did you ever leave milk and cookies out for Santa?"

"Sure, but you aren't trying to tell me Santa's a ghost, are you?"

Mandy laughed. "No. No Santa zombies. However, there's reason to believe that came from the tradition in Ireland of leaving milk on the windowsill on Christmas Eve as a way to welcome back the spirits of the family who were expected on that night. The ancient Greeks frequently made offerings of food for the dead. Or take Halloween. Everyone dresses up and goes on a candy search, but few people know the history of the holiday. It dates back to the ancient Celtic holiday of Samhain. It was believed the gates of the land of the dead were open at that time. That the barrier between the living and the dead was the thinnest on that night. People would set bonfires, leave out food offerings, and dress in costume to fool the dead."

"You're ruining what used to be a great, candy-focused holiday for me."

"Sorry about that." She smiled and tilted her head to the side. "I guess I'm trying to tell you that while it may seem strange to talk about ghosts, it wasn't always that way. It used to be a common belief, accepted. There wasn't anything odd about it. I believe the gap between the two worlds used to be smaller. There was more communication."

"So assuming there is a ghost, why am I so lucky to see things when no one else does?"

"I believe you *are* lucky," she said, missing my sarcasm. "Ghosts wait a long time to find someone open enough to hear them. They see those people as a gift. It's too bad everyone doesn't have that gift." Mandy looked almost ready to cry. All this talk about her friends was clearly getting to her. I bet she'd give anything to hear a word from her deceased friend, and I felt ashamed for sounding more spooked than honored to have a possible ghost communication.

"So you believe ghosts exist?"

"I don't believe, I know."

Her certainty surprised me. "Do you have any advice?"

Her eyes locked on to mine. "Ghosts are no different than people. There are those who are easy to understand, and those who don't speak clearly. Be sure to listen closely so you know what's being said. And be careful. Very careful."

Chapter 31

"Maybe it would work better if we lit a candle or something," Nate said, breaking the silence.

Figures. The undead bother you all the time until you finally *want* to talk to them, and then they can't bother to show up. What the heck else do they have to do in the great beyond? Am I supposed to believe they got caught up watching something on TV and lost track of time? I rolled my shoulders back. Hunching over the Ouija board that Nicole forgot at my house had left me feeling sore. So far it had given me zero messages from the other side and a backache.

"I don't get it," I said. "You would think that a spirit who wants to get a message through would take this chance to say something."

"Maybe it's me," Nate offered.

"No," I said, but I wondered if he was right. Maybe the ghost knew about his reluctance toward the whole communication project. For all I knew, ghosts were touchy and sensitive about that kind of thing. "I'm telling you, the night of the slumber party this thing worked." I gave the board a tiny shove across the floor.

"Maybe this ghost doesn't have anything else to say."

"One, two, three? I need more information than that. What am I supposed to make of numbers? That the ghost has mastered basic counting skills?" I winced as the words came out of my mouth. If the ghost was his sister, then I'd just insulted her. Evie had communication issues: she was most likely doing the best she could.

"What else do you have other than the numbers?"

"I have a few seashells and a piece of broken mirror." I shook my head. "It sounds crazy, doesn't it?"

"Get everything out, and let's look at it all together."

I got up and pulled the seashells and mirror out of the back of my underwear drawer and put them in the middle of the Ouija board. Nate picked up the piece of mirror and turned it over in his hand a few times. I tried to show him the partial image of a face, but with only a corner of an eye and the side of a cheek visible, I could tell he didn't see it. He suggested that maybe it was nothing more than damage to the silver backing on the glass. I pushed the shells around on the board until I noticed something.

"That's weird." I'd pushed the shells into three piles. One shell, two shells, three shells. "The numbers line up."

"Or it could be one pile of six," Nate said, pushing them back together.

"Hang on, there was something else." I stood back up and went to my bookshelf. I pulled out my copy of *Harry Potter* and found the torn pieces of the sketch from my first night in the house. They fluttered to the floor and Nate assembled them like puzzle pieces until the picture of the window seat was complete.

"If there's a clue here, I don't see it," Nate said.

"We must be missing something." I pushed the slips of paper closer together, trying to fill in the gaps.

Nate looked at the picture. "It's Evie's room, the way it looked when she was alive. She used to sit in that window seat all the time and look through books. My mom would read to her." Nate pointed at the book that Mr. Stripes was leaning against in the picture. "That's my mom's copy of *Alice in Wonderland*. It was her favorite story as a kid, and for a wedding present my dad gave her a first-edition copy. He lost his shit when he saw Evie looking through it once, because she had jam on her fingers. My mom said it didn't matter, that books were like stuffed animals; they were better when they were well loved—more real, more alive. She used to read it to Evie all the time. To be honest, I'm not sure how much Evie understood, but at least my mom liked it."

"Maybe there's some kind of other number message in the picture." My finger trailed along the bookshelves in the sketch.

"There are twelve books in the picture. Twelve can be divided by one, two, or three."

"Take this the nicest way, but I think you're stretching. My sister had a pretty significant cognitive delay; coming up with number and story problems wasn't exactly her thing." He sounded annoyed.

"Well, if that's not it, maybe you can think of some other idea of what all this means, or do you not want to do this at all?"

"No, I don't want to do it. This whole thing feels wrong somehow."

"I know thinking about your mom and sister upsets you."

"Then let's not do it." Nate stood and pulled me up from the floor. "Let's do something else, something fun."

"This is what I need to be doing. Something is happening to me, and I need to figure it out. You said you would help me."

"We tried to figure it out. How long are we supposed to spend on this project? This is the third night in a row I've snuck up to your room, and instead of doing anything else, we spend the entire time trying to talk to my dead sister."

I took a step back. "Whoa. That's not fair. Are you saying the only reason I should invite you up to my room is to fool around?"

"That's not what I said." Nate ran his hands through his hair. "Let's get out of here."

"And if I say no?"

"Then I'll go by myself. Tonight's the party out at the cove."

"Tell me you're joking. I thought you weren't going to go, or do you like the idea of Nicole hanging on your every word?"

"At least she's interested in what I have to say instead of wanting to hear from someone who isn't even alive anymore."

"Maybe the problem is you don't want to hear the message."

"This is bullshit. I'm leaving." Nate crossed over to the door.

"You're being a dick," I called after him.

"And you're acting crazy," Nate spit out.

I felt my face flush red-hot as if he had slapped me. Tears sprang into my eyes. His eyes went wide too, as if he had shocked himself.

"Isobel," he stuttered. "I didn't mean that. I swear to God, it just came out."

I crossed the room in three steps. "You meant it, but you're wrong. There's nothing wrong with me. Now get out." I shut the door in his face before he could say anything else. I stood with my hand pressed against the door. I could hear him tap lightly, but I didn't respond. I had the sense he was standing pressed against the other side. After a few seconds I could hear him slip down the stairs.

I slid down the door until I was sitting on the floor with my back pressed against the wood. I put my head on my knees and let myself cry.

Chapter 32

I sat there until I didn't have any tears left. The whole thing was a waste. Trying to talk to the ghost was stupid; thinking I could have a relationship with someone like Nate was even more absurd. If I wanted to take control of some part of my life the way Dr. Mike recommended, then what I needed to do was come up with a plan for getting the heck off this island. I needed to make up with Anita, who was at least a real friend.

I called Anita's phone, and her voice mail clicked on. I shook off the feeling that she had seen my number and decided not to pick it up. "Hey," I said into the phone, suddenly unsure of what to say. "I know you're ticked at me and I can't blame you, but I need to talk to you." I felt the hot fist of fresh tears threatening to spill out all over again. "Things with me aren't so good. Call when you can, okay?"

I clicked the phone off. I'd talk to Anita and that would help. I'd also ask Dr. Mike if it made sense for me to try some kind of medication. Getting help wasn't losing, it was taking control.

I was considering digging out a calendar and calculating exactly how many days were left until graduation when I noticed that the room was colder. Much colder. The hair on my arms stood up as I broke out in goose bumps.

You've to be kidding me. Now she shows up?

"You better not start that knocking again," I called out softly. "There's no need to repeat yourself after all. One, two, three. I got that part."

My eyes slid around the room as I waited to see what would happen. The room was even colder. I could see the mist of my breath in the air every time I exhaled. I pinched my thigh. This was real.

Thump.

I jumped. One of my books had fallen over on the shelf.

Thump.

Another book fell over and slid onto the floor. I pressed my back against the door and wished Nate hadn't left.

Thump

Thump

Thump

My remaining books started to fall off the shelf, onto the floor, one after the other. My clock radio next to the bed clicked on, blaring the radio.

"This is WXJZ, the voice of the island, wanting to know—who's listening tonight?" The radio clicked back off.

Thump

Thump

Thump

The numbers on the digital display began to spin around so fast that they were nothing more than a red blur.

THUMP

THUMP

THUMP

"Stop. Stop it," I begged, squeezing my eyes shut as if I could keep everything away by just not seeing it . . . and just like that, it stopped. I kept my eyes closed for a second. I opened them slowly. Every book I owned was in a pile on the floor. The cold was leaving, too. I could feel the room warming up around me, almost as if the furnace had kicked on full blast. I looked over at the radio. The time on the face was 1:23. Whatever had been in my room was gone now.

I stood up and shuffled over to the pile of books. I picked one up. It didn't look any different. It didn't feel any different. It was a copy of *The Phantom Tollbooth*. It had been one of my favorite books as a kid. My dad had gotten it for me. I turned the pages. There was a smear of what I guessed was chocolate on one of the pages. Much like Nate's mom, I came from a line of well-loved-book people who didn't mind a smear here and there. I scraped the chocolate blob off the page so the page number could be seen again.

I dropped the book. It felt like my heart had stopped. Was that it? It might be nothing, but it was the first idea that had made any sense in a long time. I looked at the clock one last time, and then I left.

I stopped at Nate's room and tapped on the door softly. Mom and Dick's room was just a few doors down, and the last thing I wanted was to wake them up. I turned the knob slowly and pushed the door open.

"Nate? Are you here?"

His room was pitch black, but even though I couldn't see very well, I could tell he wasn't there. He must have snuck out of the house and gone to the party. I didn't know if I should wait for him or check things out on my own. An image of him sitting on a piece of driftwood at the cove came into my mind. He had a beer in one hand and Nicole in the other. Forget it. I wasn't waiting for him. For all I knew, it would turn out to be nothing anyway. If I found anything, we could talk about it later.

I tiptoed down into the kitchen and grabbed the flashlight that Dick kept by the back door. I clicked it on. There wouldn't be any lights in the west wing. I stepped quietly through the foyer, listening for any sounds coming from upstairs, but everything was quiet. The west wing was cold, but normal cold, the way it should feel. There wasn't the same chilling cold that had been in my room. The smell of mildew and rot tickled my nose.

When I got to the library I closed the door behind me with a quiet click and panned the room with the flashlight to confirm I was alone. I crossed the room and checked the window. It wasn't locked. I suspected Nate had left through here to keep Dick from knowing he was out on a school night. I was half tempted to lock the window to teach him a lesson, but decided against it. I slid the thick green velvet curtains shut so that any light from the flashlight wouldn't bounce off the window, just in case Dick was looking out from upstairs. I started on the farside, trailing my finger along the shelves. I tried to figure out if there was any sort of rhyme or reason to how the books were kept, but everything seemed sort of clustered together. *Tom Sawyer* next to a Tom Clancy. A bunch of boring looking books on economics, broken up by a hardcover Calvin and Hobbes collection. They weren't even organized by size or color. There was a serious lack of the Dewey decimal system in this library. If Mandy were here she would whip this place into shape in no time.

I climbed the rolling ladder so I could check the shelves at the top of the bookcase. I heard a floorboard creak and I shut the flashlight off quickly. There was a rustle outside the door. I pressed against the ladder, my face between two rungs, and tried to hold my breath. I must have breathed in some dust, because instantly I wanted to sneeze. I wriggled my nose back and forth to make the urge go away. My ears strained to pick up any other sounds, but I didn't hear anything. It must have been the house settling or maybe a mouse. I refused to think rat.

Unless whatever was out in the hallway was being quiet so it could listen too.

I shook off the heebie-jeebies. I had to stop winding myself up. There was enough creepy stuff going on without asking for more. I let out a tiny sneeze, but no one called out. I slowed my breathing and counted to a hundred.

Nothing.

I clicked the flashlight back on and waited to see if Dick would fling open the door and demand to know what I was doing, but it stayed quiet. I turned my attention back to the shelves. The only things on the top shelves were books I was pretty sure no one had read for decades and a gray flannel blanket of dust. I sneezed again and almost dropped the flashlight but caught it just in time in the crook of my arm. I shivered at the idea of losing my light, and hurried to examine the last row of shelves.

I was about a third of the way down the next shelf when I saw it, a book with greenish-tan binding and red detail. I slid the book out. *Alice's Adventures in Wonderland*. The cover had an illustration of Alice being attacked by a wall of playing cards.

I sat down in one of the leather chairs. I couldn't tell if I wanted to find anything or not. I opened the cover and thumbed through the first few pages. I thought the book might smell a bit musty, but it didn't. The book opened to an illustration of Alice following the white rabbit. I flipped ahead to page 123.

The pages were stuck together, and I didn't want to tear them. This first-edition book probably cost more than I could imagine. Dick could probably tell me to the penny what this thing was worth. While Nate's mom might have been a fan of letting books be broken in and loved, I was pretty sure Dick would make me pay him back for any lost value if I so much as sneezed on a page. I slid my finger between the pages, slowly breaking them apart.

The pages fell open. There were two pieces of paper tucked in between pages 122 and 123.

Chapter 33

I unfolded the papers. The first was a statement from Bank of America. It had Dick's name on the account, but the address was a PO box over on the mainland. Interesting. I'd seen bank statements come here to the house. Either he had closed this account and opened one with the bank here on the island, or he had a separate account. I checked the date on the statement; it was the month before the boating accident. I wondered why Nate's mom wasn't on the account. The account had just over $100,000 in it. That was a nice chunk of change.

The second paper was a printout of an email, with a number scribbled at the bottom of the page. I checked the date; it was in early February, right around the time of the boating accident. I read through the email quickly.

Dear Ms. Wickham,

In response to your call to our office inquiring as to the diminished balance in the account, we confirm that funds in the amount of $543,000.00 were transferred from the trust account set up for your daughter, Evelyn Wickham, to an account in your husband's name. These withdrawals occurred over a period of seven years, starting immediately after the settlement was determined in your daughter's case.

Your request for money to be transferred to Progressive Rehab to cover the costs for a therapist to work with Evelyn has to be denied at this time, as there are not sufficient funds to cover this withdrawal. The account currently has a balance of $5,550.00. Copies of the monthly statements can be provided at your request.

The trust for your daughter was set up in both your and your husband's names following the settlement from the malpractice case. You each hold independent signing authority for these funds. The signed releases for each withdrawal are available for your review if desired. As to what these monies were used for, I am unable to comment, as we have no way to track the funds following them leaving the trust.

While I understand your distress, I can assure you this firm has acted in accordance with both the law and the confines of the trust agreement. If you were unaware of these withdrawals, I respectfully suggest that you and your husband,

Mr. Wickham, discuss this in more detail. If there is anything further we can do, please do not hesitate to contact our office.

Sincerely,
Brian Hudson
Hudson, Vickers, and Ackerly Law Firm

Holy shit. I folded up both pieces of paper and tucked them back into the book. Talk about going down the rabbit hole. My heart was beating quickly as I started to run through the logic in my head.

1. Dick had a private account.
2. Dick spent his daughter's settlement money without telling his wife, and no one other than Dick seemed to know where the money went.
3. Sylvia, Dick's first wife, didn't find out about this until just before her death.

My mind leaped to a possible number four: Sylvia confronted Dick about the missing money and he killed her over it. I wasn't a homicide detective or anything, but I watched enough *Law & Order* to know that over half a million dollars provided at least 500,000 motives for murder.

I unfolded the paper again and looked at the number someone

had scrawled at the bottom. There wasn't a name written down, but it was a Seattle number. It seemed familiar, but I couldn't place it.

I stuck the book under my arm and slipped out of the library. The house was still deathly silent. I put the flashlight back in the kitchen. I looked at the phone and debated my options. It made more sense to wait until tomorrow. Nate would be home, plus my call wouldn't wake anyone up. On the other hand, I was never known for my ability to delay gratification. I picked up the phone and dialed before I could think about it anymore, and hoped whoever owned the number was the kind of person who liked to stay up late.

I was prepared to tell whoever answered that I must have dialed wrong, but it wasn't a personal line. A business voice mail picked up. As soon as I heard the voice on the line, the blood ran out of my head and I could feel a cold wet sweat break out.

"You've reached the office of White, Watts, and Kleinmann. Our office is now closed. If you know the extension of the party you want to reach, you may press it now."

I hung up and slid down the cabinets until I was sitting on the floor. The voice on the machine was my mom's. The reason the number was familiar was because it was the main line of the law firm she used to work for. They must have left her out-of-office message on the machine even though she had quit a month ago when Dick proposed. White, Watts, and Kleinmann was a law firm that specialized in one area: divorce.

It bothered me that my mom married Dick so quickly after meeting him, but now I realized there was something that might bother me more. What if my mom knew Dick when he was still married? What if they'd been dating for a long time? And if I believed there was a chance Dick was somehow involved with his wife's murder, what did it mean if he and my mom were already a couple? Thinking your creepy stepdad might be involved in murder was one thing. Thinking your mom might be was a different thing altogether.

Dr. Mike had made it sound like taking control of my life would be a good thing. We never covered what it would mean to take control of something you wished you never knew.

Chapter 34

I waited up until close to one a.m., but Nate didn't come home. I knew he was annoyed, but I couldn't imagine he would do something with Nicole to get back at me. On the other hand, I did believe it was very possible that Nicole would tackle him if she could. If Nate was in a weakened state from beer, she could sneak up on him and pounce. I could picture her sidling up to him while the *Jaws* theme music played.

I finally crawled upstairs and into bed, but all I could do was stare at the ceiling. I was tired, but I couldn't sleep. My brain was racing like a coked-up hamster on a well-oiled rodent wheel. There was, of course, another conclusion one could leap to. I had just about convinced myself that there wasn't anything wrong with me, but I needed to show the papers to Nate to see if he would have the same reaction I did. If he didn't see anything sinister in it, then there was a chance I was having paranoid delusions. With my genetic makeup, delusions were not a good thing, but the papers had to mean something. Something had led me to the exact place to find them; that couldn't be in my head.

Anita had taught me how to do visualization and deep breathing. At the time, I'd mocked her, but at the moment, being able to relax even slightly seemed like a great idea. But the "breathe in through the nose and out through the mouth" thing wasn't working.

Or maybe it did work, because it seemed as if I closed my eyes for a second, but when I rolled over and looked at the clock, my heart stopped. I was late for school! I jumped out of bed and stood in the middle of the room trying to figure out what to do first. Another look at the clock confirmed it; I wasn't going to have time for a shower. A quick swipe of deodorant was going to have to do. I yanked on a pair of jeans and a shirt and pulled my hair into a ponytail. I looked in the mirror. Yikes. I put on some lipstick and mascara. It helped a bit, but there was no risk anyone was going to think I was a beauty pageant contestant who had wandered into school by accident.

I stuffed the copy of *Alice in Wonderland* into my backpack and ran down the stairs. Dick came out of the kitchen.

"Ah, it's you. I thought perhaps with all that noise that a herd of circus elephants had broken free from their paddock and were thundering down the stairs." Dick had a smear of jam on his upper lip. He was smiling at me.

Ever since our fight he'd redoubled his efforts to come across as my closest buddy. The day after, he'd made a big show of apologizing to me in front of my mom. That way he could be the good guy and I could be the difficult moody one. Now that I knew about the papers, I had to fight the urge to push him away from me.

"There was something for you in the mail this morning." Dick passed me an envelope. The return address was blank and the envelope looked rumpled. I peered at the postmark. The letter had been mailed from Oregon. It was from my dad. I stuffed the letter in my bag before anyone tried to take it from me.

"Thanks." I gave him a thin-lipped smile and looked around him into the kitchen. Thank God, Nate was back.

"Can I grab a ride with you?" I asked him.

Nate looked up from his bowl of cereal. "Sure. Let me finish breakfast and we'll go."

I stood by the kitchen door with my bag.

"Someone is eager to start her school day. Come on in and I'll make you some toast," Dick said.

"No, thanks." I shifted my weight and tried to send thought waves into Nate's brain.

"Breakfast is the most important meal of the day. Jump-starts the brain." Dick waved a piece of bread in my face.

"Richard, don't pick on her," my mom said.

When did Dick become the toast pimp? Did he feel some sort of need to shove carbs onto other people? The last thing I was going to do was take anything from that guy. For all I knew it would have arsenic in it. People who displeased Dick were suspiciously accident prone.

"I don't want any breakfast."

"Oh, come on, just a nibble. You're getting too skinny." Dick poked me in the waist and I slapped his hand away.

The smack sounded very loud in the kitchen. Everyone stopped what they were doing.

"Oh, Isobel," my mom said sadly.

"I don't want him touching me," I said.

Dick's eyes filled with crocodile tears. "Emotional outbursts. They talked about this."

"Who talked about what?" I asked.

"Why didn't you tell me you dropped out of cheerleading?" my mom asked.

"I was going to tell you."

Mom's and Dick's eyes met across the kitchen. Mom wiped her hands on the kitchen towel. "We've made an appointment for you in Seattle." She raised her hand before I could say anything. "This isn't open for discussion."

I looked at Dick. I knew what he was doing, getting rid of me.

Nate tipped his cereal bowl so he could drink the last of the milk. "Let's go."

"Do you want to drive?" Nate asked as we got out to the car.

"No, I need to talk to you, and I'm not sure I can talk and focus on the road at the same time."

Nate touched my arm. "Don't worry about this stupid appointment. Anyone who meets you can tell you're fine."

I waved off his comment; for once my mental health wasn't my biggest worry. By the time I jumped into the passenger seat, I was ready to explode. I pulled my dad's letter out from my bag and opened it with shaking hands. It was short.

Dearest Isobel,

I love you. Always have, always will. Call me collect anytime you want to talk. I've been listening with my heart before you ever opened your mouth.

Love, Dad

His number was scribbled at the bottom. I folded it carefully and put it in my pocket. I wanted it close to me.

Nate slammed the door as he climbed into the driver's seat. There was so much I needed to tell him that I didn't know where to start. The words were logjammed in my throat. How do you tell the guy you like that you think his dad might be a murderer? He looked over at me before he turned the key.

"Listen, I'm sorry about last night. I shouldn't have taken off like that." Nate chewed on his lower lip.

It took me a beat to realize what he was talking about. So much had happened since then, I'd almost forgotten how we left things.

"It doesn't matter," I said.

"No, it does. I don't want to be one of those people who runs away from conflict instead of dealing with it."

I opened my mouth to say something, but he cut me off.

"I went to the party last night." He tilted his head back. "You were right. It was a mistake."

"I'm serious. It doesn't matter."

"Nicole kissed me."

I felt my brain screech to a halt. WTF? "She kissed you," I repeated. So was he saying that he didn't kiss her back?

"We were sitting there just talking, and then she leaned over and kissed me." He turned to face me. "I pushed her back right away."

"What did Nicole do?"

"She wasn't happy."

"She's not the kind of girl who's used to a lot of noes."

"I don't care what she thinks. I care what *you* think. Nothing happened, but I wanted you to hear this from me and not someone at school." He tilted my chin up with his finger. "I'd never lie to you."

"I know," I whispered back, and somehow I *did* know. Nate was like someone from another time. He was one of those people who meant it when he gave you his word. His character mattered to him. I would totally have smothered him with kisses to show him what a stand-up kind of guy I thought he was, except for the fact that we were still parked in our driveway.

"What did you want to tell me?" he asked.

"I figured it out."

"Figured what out?"

"The one, two, three thing."

Nate read my expression. "It's bad, isn't it?"

I nodded.

"Is it my dad? Is he doing it?"

I looked past Nate to see Dick peering at us through the living room curtains. I had the eerie feeling that somehow he could tell what we were talking about. "I'll tell you later. Can you go now?" I hunched down in my seat. Nate turned around and saw his dad in the window and then glanced back at me.

"Okay. You can tell me on the way."

I waited until we were past the orchard and turning onto the main road. Then I took a deep breath and jumped in.

"It wasn't one, two, three; it was one twenty-three."

Nate parked in the back of the student lot. He had asked a few questions when I started, but he hadn't said anything for the past few minutes. The car was off, but he sat looking straight out the windshield, his hands at ten and two on the steering wheel. I watched everyone streaming into school. It was raining, so everyone was rushing. With umbrellas and their hoods up it was hard to tell who anyone was.

"Are you sure, Isobel? Maybe it wasn't what it looked like," Nate said, breaking the silence at last. His voice was tight and thin.

"I brought everything." I fished through my bag and pulled out the book. Nate's hand hovered over it as if he wasn't sure if he wanted to touch it. I opened the book myself and pulled out the papers, handing them over.

Nate looked over the pages, flipping back and forth. His finger traced over the writing at the bottom of the one page.

"I remember my mom talking about this treatment, just before . . ." His voice trailed off for a beat. "Just before she died. It was a one-on-one therapy that was supposed to reestablish neural pathways or some such thing. She was really excited for Evie to try it. She figured Evie was so young that her brain would be more open to change, more flexible or something."

"It looks like she went to get money for the treatment, only to find out it was missing."

"It wasn't missing; my dad took it. He stole that money right out from under my mom and sister."

I could see his jaw tighten like he was grinding his teeth together. I rested my hand on his arm. "Do you know what your dad spent the money on?"

"If I had to guess, it would be the house. The whole place is a giant money pit. The wiring is old; the plumbing is even older. There's always wood rot, or the roof is leaking something. My dad's been saying for years that if he didn't do something soon with the west wing, it was really going to start falling apart. I never asked where he was getting the money to chip away at things. My mom wanted to sell it. There were people a few years ago who wanted to buy the place and turn it into an inn with a spa and everything. I remember my parents fighting about it. My mom wanted to buy a regular house."

"Something without a ballroom?"

Nate smiled. "At least a smaller ballroom."

"There's more," I said. "The phone number scribbled at the bottom is an attorney's office. The firm specializes in divorce. It's the biggest one in Seattle. Really well-known. My mom used to work there."

Nate looked up, surprised. "Do you think my mom and your mom knew each other?"

"I don't know. If your mom called this firm, then my mom would have at least talked to her on the phone. She was the receptionist there."

"If my mom knew my dad took Evie's money, she'd consider getting a divorce. They already didn't have a great relationship. My mom was a major momma bear when it came to my sister. She would have done anything for her. She blamed herself for Evie's accident. I think she thought she should have been able to do something. After she was born, Evie was in the hospital for months, and it was pretty clear that she wasn't ever going to be normal. The doctors mentioned the option of putting my sister in some kind of home. My mom lost it. She was never going to let that happen."

"She sounds like she was a great mom," I said softly.

"Yeah." Nate took several deep breaths, and I could tell he was trying hard not to cry. "She would have left my dad when she heard this. There would have been no 'I'm sorry' big enough to make up for it. So I can understand how she'd run into your mom, but how did your mom and my dad meet? I can tell you my mom wouldn't have been in the mood to make any introductions."

"I've been thinking about that. Our parents say they met in June, but what if they didn't? What if they were together before your mom passed away? If your dad had known she was talking to a lawyer, he could have called the law firm, too, looking for information."

"You think they were having an affair?"

"Maybe. I wondered . . . what if my mom knew your mom was looking for a divorce?"

"Then if your mom told my dad . . . He can be pretty charming when he wants information."

"Yep."

Nate shook his head. "Then what? Do you think your mom and my dad conspired to kill my mom? That's stupid. People get divorced all the time. I'm not saying it's a good thing, but there would be no reason to kill anyone."

"If your parents got divorced, would your dad have to sell

the house? I mean, would your mom want to split it so she'd have money to take care of Evie?"

Nate slumped in his seat. He looked like a balloon that someone had let half the air out of.

"I hadn't thought of that. My dad would never sell the house. Never. He loves that house more than anything—me, my sister, my mom."

I hated to see Nate like this. He looked lost, alone. I slid closer to him in my seat. "I'm thinking out loud. I'm not sure of anything. I could be way off base."

Nate didn't say anything. He was staring down at his hands on his lap as if they were a crystal ball that was going to have the answer to this mess.

"Or maybe my mom and your dad did know each other, but nothing happened," I suggested. I had been desperate to talk to Nate, to tell him this news, but now that I had, I wanted to take it all back. This is what everyone talks about when they say if you unburden yourself, you're shoving the burden onto someone else. "Or, you know, it could also be one of those things where the whole thing is just one of those random coincidences. You hear about that stuff all the time. Once I read this story about these guys who lived next door to each other and both had wives with the same name, and it turned out they were twins who'd been separated at birth."

Nate looked up at me, and I forced myself to stop talking.

"You're right. This paper doesn't have to mean anything, but it does. If we'd just found it in a desk, that might be something, but you found it because my sister, my dead sister, is sending messages from the beyond to lead us to it."

I didn't say anything. He had a point.

"My sister is trying to tell us something. She tried to tell me, and I didn't listen. I was so impatient that I had to go to a party." Nate slapped his hand on the steering wheel. I rested my hand on his arm.

"Don't be so hard on yourself. It wasn't like you didn't try."

"But instead of sticking with it, I quit. Just like my dad. He never had any patience for Evie. He used to get annoyed when she was trying to say something, and he'd cut her off or make a guess about what she wanted to say, or he'd pass her off to my mom."

"You're nothing like your dad." I rubbed his shoulder, wishing I could do something more to make it okay.

Nate pulled me into his arms and buried his head in my neck.

"You are the best thing to happen to me in a long time," he said.

"It's going to be okay," I whispered back. I wasn't really sure how, but it seemed like the right thing to say.

Nate pulled back and smiled. He brushed the hair out of my eyes. "We're going to figure this out."

"Of course we are. We're going to figure it out together."

He leaned in and kissed me. He smelled like shampoo. Apparently, I find that smell very sexy, because as soon as I took a deep breath of it, I found myself pulling him back to me, kissing him harder and deeper. The cologne companies could make zillions if they knew the average teen girl was so excited by the smell of clean. It wasn't that I wanted to kiss Nate; I wanted to crawl into his lap and melt into his body. It seemed like he must have been feeling the same thing. He had one hand wrapped in my hair and the other was on my side, moving into boob cupping territory. If there hadn't been the parking brake between us, we would have had to have a conversation about using protection. It was amazing.

Then everything went to hell.

Chapter 35

Despite the facts that I was practically straddling the parking brake and it was getting cold in the car, the kiss might have been the best one I'd ever had. You read in books stuff about "waves of passion" and "burning loins," but I'd pretty much figured that was fiction. Who even talks about their loins in normal life? But this kiss was making me very aware of my loins, and they were definitely on fire.

The sight of Nicole staring at us through the windshield with her eyes and mouth wide-open put my loin fire out quick. I yanked back from Nate. I don't know why. It was already too late. She'd seen us. There was no way to make this situation look casual. What was I going to say? Nate was looking for his car keys in my mouth with his tongue? I sat back, frozen in my seat.

"Oh shit," Nate said, summarizing the situation perfectly.

I could see Nicole standing there in the rain, taking these deep breaths like she was trying to keep from blowing up or was a yoga teacher gone rabid. She looked to me like she was at risk of hyperventilating. Without saying anything, she spun around and started marching toward school. I jumped out of the car and ran after her.

"Nicole, wait a second, I can explain." I reached out and grabbed her by the elbow. She turned around, her face screwed up into a grimace.

"Don't touch me. Well, I guess I know now why you didn't want to help me hook up with Nate. You're the kind of person who likes to keep things in the family," she snarled. I stepped back as if she'd slapped me. "I thought we were friends, and then you stab me in the back."

"How did I stab you in the back?"

"Do you throw yourself into the arms of all your friends' boyfriends?"

Nate walked up. "Chill out. You and I never dated. She didn't tell you about us, but we weren't planning on telling anyone."

"That's incest, you know. And it's disgusting."

"We're not actually related," I stressed.

"Don't feel like you have to explain anything to her. We haven't done anything wrong." Nate stepped closer to me, his hand resting on my lower back.

"The fact that you don't recognize how wrong it is shows just how messed up your family is," Nicole said to Nate. Then she turned to me. "I guess I shouldn't be too surprised at anything you do. The crazy are supposed to be unbalanced."

"What are you talking about?" I asked.

"You think I didn't know you were seeing my dad? The heating vent in his office is connected directly to my room. Most of the time I can't stand to listen to all his whiny patients talk about their feelings and how life is so hard because their mommies were mean to them, but I have to hand it to you. Your story is better than cable TV. Crazy dad, shaky grip on reality . . . You're more screwed up than anyone on this island." Nicole barked out a laugh. "Well, I guess you're no more fucked-up than the guy you're fucking."

Nate stepped closer so his face was in Nicole's. "Shut your mouth."

Her lips slammed together. She tossed her hair over her shoulder.

"You don't need to tell me to shut up. I don't have anything to say to either of you." She looked us both up and down as if we were something nasty she found on the bottom of her shoe, and then she spun around and walked into school.

"We are totally screwed," I said softly as I watched her walk away.

"No, we're not. We haven't done anything wrong."

"That's not how it's going to sound when she tells everyone."

I noticed that Nate didn't bother to disagree with me. Even he knew nothing was going to stop Nicole from telling the entire student body—heck, the entire island, maybe most of the

Northwestern US if she could—that he and I were together and that I was certifiably crazy.

"It doesn't matter." Nate took my hand and started to walk toward the door.

I took a deep breath and told myself he was right. We weren't related, and while dating your stepbrother might not be exactly "common," it wasn't illegal. It wasn't like we'd grown up with each other. And who listens through the vents in their house to their dad's office? Sounded to me like Nicole was the one with issues. Besides, with the exception of Nate, I didn't care what anyone thought of me.

Chapter 36

How to tell if you have social leprosy:

1. When you walk into a room, instead of smiling and saying hello, your fellow classmates all stop talking and stare at you like they've never seen anything quite like you. When you walk away, you can hear them all talking again.

2. If you accidentally trip in gym class and do a face-plant on the basketball court, instead of anyone helping you up, you'll hear them snicker. Someone may say, loud enough for you to hear, "nice one."

3. As you walk down the hallway, there's a three-

foot barrier between you and everyone else, as if your loser status were as contagious as Ebola.

4. Even the hot-lunch lady shakes her head in disgust when she sees you, and she's been wearing the same pants with crusted-on baked beans since the beginning of the year.

I had to hand it to Nicole. She was better at spreading information than the emergency broadcast system. Near as I could tell, by third period everyone in school knew Nicole's version of events. I took my lunch tray from the hot lunch lady (who had no business judging me) and stood looking out over the cafeteria. Anyone who met my eyes looked away.

"Come on. We can sit over there."

I felt a huge wave of relief as I realized Nate was behind me. He motioned to a table near the window, and I trailed after him. There were two juniors sitting there, but when they saw Nate and me come over, they jumped up from the table.

"You don't mind if we join you, do you?" Nate plopped his lunch sack down and, without waiting for them to answer, dropped himself into the seat. They scurried away without saying anything, looking over their shoulders as if they thought we might be chasing them down. "Guess they were done with their lunch." Nate pulled his sandwich out and then looked up at me. "Are you still getting hot lunch? Talk about a slow learner."

"I didn't make anything this morning. I had other stuff on my mind." I shifted from foot to foot. "Maybe we shouldn't eat in here."

"Why not?" Nate asked, his mouth full of sandwich.

"Are you telling me you haven't noticed we've become the social lepers of Nairne High?"

"I noticed. I just don't care." Nate pushed the chair next to him away from the table with his foot so I could sit down. "If you ask me, what that lunch is going to do to your internal organs is a much bigger concern than what people here think of you."

I looked down at the tray. There was some sort of square piece of grayish meat covered in gravy. I poked it with my fork. I couldn't think of a single animal that came in a square shape, which left me with the uncomfortable image of some sort of meat press that stamped out uniformly square chunks of meat made out of things like beaks and hooves. Nate tore off half of his sandwich and passed it to me.

"If you keep this up, I'm going to have to start making extra sandwiches for my lunches so I won't waste away," he said.

"You had to give me your lunch twice. It's not exactly a radical starvation program I've got you on." I shoved the sandwich in my mouth before he could take it back.

Nate looked over his shoulder and then leaned in. "About what we were talking about in the car, I think we should go to the police."

The sandwich stuck in my throat and I had to force it down. "The cops? Are you sure?"

"No." Nate ran his hand through his hair. "The whole situation makes me sick, but I don't know what else to do."

I chewed on the inside of my mouth. "I don't think it's a good idea. If we go to the police, they're going to talk to your dad and he'll deny everything."

"We'll show them the bank statement and the email."

"And your dad will have an answer for it. He's a big guy on this island. They're going to look at me and see someone who has a lot of crazy in the family, is already seeing a therapist, whose parents are taking her for an evaluation with a residential treatment center, and has made it pretty clear I didn't want to move here. The cops are going to blame me."

"We'll tell them how you found the stuff."

"Oh, that will convince them. Make sure you mention how I'm getting messages from your deceased sister. The police love stuff like that." I rubbed my temple. I liked Nate, but we saw the world differently. He came from a background where the police were all Officer Friendly types. It wasn't that I was on the wrong side of the law, but I knew enough to know that cops were influenced by stuff like how much money you have and if your parents donate to the Police Charity Drive. There were plenty of times in Seattle when I'd be doing nothing more than walking down the street, and a cop car would slow down and follow me for a while before they got out to ask me where was I headed and what I was up to.

I knew exactly how a meeting with the police would go. Dick would shake his head sadly and mention my mental difficulties and how I didn't seem to be managing the transition well. My mom would disown me for causing more trouble in her perfect marriage, and it would be the final nail in my coffin. I'd be locked up before the day was over. Nate would stick up for me, but everyone would decide that he was blinded by sex and depression over losing his mom and sister. The fall guy in this situation would be me. No way they would believe me over Dick, no way.

"If you don't want to go to the cops, what do you want to do, confront him?" Nate asked.

"I don't see that going well either. He's just going to say he had nothing to do with it."

"We can't ignore the situation either."

"We need proof," I insisted.

"Okay, Sherlock Holmes, what are we going to do? Try out some forensic techniques? Maybe go through the attic and see if we can find my uncle's old college microscope? Look for fingerprints?"

I sat back in the chair. Nate was pissed. His hands were clenched in fists, and I could see his lips pressed into a tight line. Suddenly the saying about not shooting the messenger was making sense. "Don't be mad at me," I said.

"I'm not," Nate spit out.

"Could have fooled me."

"Okay, I'm pissed. Not at you; at the whole situation. Do you realize what we're talking about? About what all this means?" He looked around the cafeteria to make sure no one was listening in and then leaned closer. "If we're right, my dad, maybe with help from your mom, murdered my mom and sister. Murder. We can't sit on that information. We have to do something. I know Deputy Burrows. He used to coach my Little League team. He'll listen to us."

Deputy Little League might listen, but I knew that was a long way from believing. The problem was, I was lacking a plan B. I didn't know what else we should do. Nate was right that I didn't have the slightest clue how to get any evidence to back up what we were saying.

"Can you wait a day?"

"What's a day going to do?"

"I don't know. I need some time to think, and maybe there's a way to get more proof." I shrugged. "Once we start talking, there's no way to take it back. We're not going to get a do-over. I know you trust Deputy Burrows, but I don't know him. We've waited this long. Would a day or two more really matter?"

Nate sighed. "No, a day isn't going to change anything. We're running out of time, though. They've arranged an appointment for you in Seattle for Friday. Promise me you won't do anything stupid."

"Thanks for the vote of confidence. I'd been planning to

come up with the most moronic plan I could think of, but I guess now I won't. ”

"I mean it, Isobel. If you go head-to-head with my dad, you won't win."

"I know." What I didn't say was that I wasn't planning to go head-to-head. I was going to hopefully sneak up on him somehow. I just needed to figure out how. And I needed to figure it out quickly.

Chapter 37

I slumped down in my seat. Ms. Raymond never started class on time. She was always fumbling with her papers or trying to find her glasses. I'd pictured scientist types as being more organized than Ms. Raymond. I was willing to bet you never see NASA scientists with toilet paper on their shoes. I was doodling on my notebook, trying to figure out some kind of plan to deal with Dick that didn't involve:

1. Telling the police, who weren't going to believe us
2. Confronting Dick directly, since he was never going to confess
3. Completing a college degree in criminal justice in order to be able to prove what happened.

It was hard enough to think of a plan without having to deal with Nicole. Her lab table was across the room, but there was no mistaking who she was talking about. She was surrounded by a bunch of people, including Brit and Sam. There would be whispering, and then everyone would turn to look at me. I wondered if this was how animals in the zoo felt. I was a one-woman freak of nature exhibit. I put my hand in my pocket so I could feel my dad's letter. I tried to act as though I didn't notice everyone clucking about me and instead was focused on reviewing my notes. We had to give presentations in class today. I was supposed to talk for five minutes about diabetes, but everything I'd prepared was pushed out of my mind by the odd word here and there I heard coming from their table: *crazy, psych ward, disgusting, her own brother.*

Finally Ms. Raymond told everyone to take his or her seat. Sam walked toward my lab table on the way to hers. She paused, shifting from foot to foot.

"I tried to warn you to watch out for Nicole," she said quietly. "She ruins people who cross her." Sam slipped past me and sat down.

I sat staring at the scarred lab table. Generations of kids had carved their names into the top. My finger traced one of the names. I kept thinking about what Sam had said about Nicole having the power to destroy people. Did she, or did we give her the power? For years I'd acted as though my mom had the power to keep me from my dad, but the truth is I hadn't wanted the hassle, so I let her. I had the power to destroy my life and the power to take it back. I felt my stomach tense as I raised my hand.

"I want to do my presentation first," I said as I stood. I didn't bother bringing my notes up with me. I wasn't going to need them.

Ms. Raymond looked surprised. Our class wasn't exactly full of volunteers for most things, and so far this year I hadn't set myself apart as a star student. I could hear a low murmur of whispers as I walked to the front of the room.

"My topic was diabetes, but I've changed it." I stopped to take a deep breath and looked around the room, being sure to meet Nicole's eyes. "I'm going to talk about schizophrenia." Someone in the back of the room actually gasped as if I had announced I was going to talk about penile implants.

"I don't know the numbers for schizophrenia, but mental health problems are common. Something like one in three people will have some sort of mental health problem in their life. This is a subject I know a lot about because my dad has schizophrenia."

I looked around the room, but everyone refused to meet my eyes.

"Common symptoms of the disease are hallucinations, delusions, disorganized speech, and behavior that is described as bizarre. Unlike what most people think, schizophrenia isn't the same as multiple personality disorder. Other misconceptions are that people with this disease are violent or more likely to commit crimes. This isn't true.

"Schizophrenia can typically be controlled with medications and psychological support. My dad has had the condition since I was a kid. He may have schizophrenia, but that isn't what controls his life. He's an artist, and one of the best ones I've ever seen. I'm proud he's my dad, and I'm proud of all of him, disease included, because it's a part of who he is.

"Doctors aren't sure if schizophrenia is genetic. They know that most people who develop it do so either as a teen or in their early twenties. They do know that people who have a schizophrenic parent are more likely to develop the disease, but it doesn't mean they will for sure. I don't know if I'll get it or not, but I do know that if I do, I hope I handle it with the same courage as my dad.

"Schizophrenia is a disease. No different from cancer or MS or diabetes. The only reason people are ashamed of mental health conditions is because they let people convince them they should be. Anyone who makes fun of someone with a mental health condition is low. They might as well make fun of some kid with cerebral palsy." I stared directly at Nicole. "If you ask me, people with mental health issues have nothing to be ashamed of; the people who find something funny in it do."

No one said anything. A few kids were staring at me with their mouths open, and a lot of people were staring at their desks. It looked like Sam was crying in the back. Ms. Raymond stopped shuffling her papers for once and simply smiled at me.

"That was excellent, Isobel," she said.

I gave her a nod and was ready to go back to my table when a kid raised his hand. "My mom's had depression. She takes medication for it." He looked surprised to realize he'd said it out loud.

Someone in the back called out, "My uncle's bipolar."

"My cousin has an anxiety disorder," someone else said.

"Hell, I must be crazy with all the stuff going on in my brain," said Luke from the football team, and almost everyone laughed as he stood up and took a bow.

"If he's crazy, then you better count me in too," Gary said, giving Luke a high five.

Nicole and Brit didn't meet anyone's eyes; they stared straight ahead. Sam looked like she was developing her own anxiety disorder. Her hands were twisting back and forth and her eyes kept darting around at everyone else in the room and then back to Nicole. Nicole's mouth trembled and her hands were clenched into a knot on the desk.

I walked slowly back to my seat with my head held high and my shoulders back. Not only had I put Nicole in her place, but I felt proud of myself, and I was pretty sure I'd nailed an A+ on the presentation. Not too bad.

Chapter 38

The rest of the day passed without any hassles. In fact, a lot of people smiled at me in the hall or made a point to say hello. It would have been a perfect afternoon if only I could have come up with some idea of what I was going to do with the Dick problem. I checked my phone for the one millionth time. Still no message from Anita. I was going to have to talk this through with someone else.

I turned down a ride from Nate after school and walked over to the library instead. The cranky librarian was at her usual place, sort of hunched over the checkout desk, looking around waiting for someone to deface a book. She looked like the kind of person who liked to collect fines in the form of waterboarding. For the life of me I couldn't figure out why the town paid to have two librarians on staff at all times. I'd never been in there when they were dealing with a crowd. It wasn't like there was a long line of people all pushing and shoving to get their literary needs met.

I found Mandy in her usual spot in the stacks. She smiled when she saw me.

"You look happy," she said.

"Today was one of those days that started off lousy, but ended good."

"How are things going?" She turned her head to the side. It didn't seem like an idle question. It felt like she was really interested.

I plopped down in a seat. I really needed to talk to someone who wasn't involved in the situation. It felt like things were spinning out of control and I could use some help in figuring out what to do. I'd hoped Anita would have called, but she must still have been ticked. Mandy seemed like my best option, and with the librarian code of silence, I was pretty sure she wouldn't blab to anyone. So much had happened since I saw her last that I wasn't even sure where to begin. I explained how we'd tried to contact the ghost, but hadn't had any luck at first, but then found the book with the documents in it. I told her how Nate and I suspected our parents had known each other before the accident, and that our big fear is that they may have been involved in what happened, but we didn't have any way to prove it and I was certain Dick was putting plans in place to get rid of me. "And Nate wants to go to the police, but . . ." My voice trailed off.

"You're afraid the police won't believe you, especially since the Wickham family has so much money and prestige here on the island."

"You're going to tell me I'm being stupid and should trust the justice system."

"No. You're right. I know the Wickham family is responsible for a lot of things. When those girls disappeared, do you know what happened? They fell through a rotted well cover. The first girl was killed when she fell, but the other girl was alive. Scared, hungry, hurt, but alive. She called for help, and just when she was starting to give up hope, someone came. He looked down that well, saw her there, and then slid a new piece of wood across the top. He left her down there because he didn't like anyone on his land, he didn't want to be sued because the well cover hadn't been fixed, and he knew he'd get away with it. And he did get away with it. By the time the police searched the property, she couldn't call for help anymore because she was dead too. They never found those girls." Her voice was low, but I could feel the waves of anger coming off in every word.

"Wait, how could you know all of that?"

She shrugged and looked out the window. "Only someone there would know, but that's my theory."

While I appreciated that she felt she could tell me things, I had enough mysteries to solve without worrying about if Dick had killed anyone else twenty years ago. I sighed in frustration. "I still don't know what to do."

"You need to get Richard Wickham to confess to what he did."

"I know, but I don't know how to do that. It's not like if I ask him, he's going to roll over and spill his guts, just because I asked. He's not afraid of me."

Mandy smiled. "I think you've put your finger on it. Everyone is afraid of something, and fear can drive people to do a lot of things they wouldn't otherwise do. What is Richard afraid of?"

"I don't know." I sighed again. Mandy didn't say anything. I knew this was one of those situations where I was supposed to come up with the answer on my own. I tried to think. "He wouldn't be afraid of the police, because he'll figure they'd believe him."

"So who would he be afraid of? Who makes him nervous?"

I chewed on my thumbnail while I thought about it. I couldn't really think of anyone. The one benefit of being as arrogant as Dick is that he assumes everyone loves him, and if they seem not to like him he chalks it up to jealousy. I'd never seen him be intimidated by anyone. The only person I could remember him talking about with any sort of awe was his mom. It was clear his mom wasn't exactly the cuddly sort who met him after school with graham crackers and milk. She was more of the "whack you on the back of the hands with a ruler and tell you to suck it up" sort. She'd be a great one to help me, except for the fact that she'd been dead for years. Figures. I had one ghost to help me, but not the one I needed.

My mouth fell open. That was it. The idea was insane, but

I was starting to appreciate a bit of crazy in my life. It was just crazy enough that it might work.

"I think I know what to do," I said, clapping my hands together.

"Shh." The cranky librarian was standing at the end of the aisle, glaring down at me. "You are aware this is a library, aren't you?"

I shot a look over at Mandy to see if she would say anything, but she stayed quiet with a small smile on her face. I had the sense she was used to random outbursts of library rule enforcement.

"I'm sorry if we were loud," I said.

"We?" She raised one eyebrow.

I managed to avoid rolling my eyes. "I meant sorry if *I* was loud. It won't happen again."

"The library is open to everyone, but if you continue to disturb patrons, I'm going to have to ask you to leave."

She was acting like I had been practicing my bongo drums in the reference section instead of having a simple conversation with another librarian.

"I promise to keep quiet from now on," I said, holding up my right hand like I was taking an oath.

The librarian stared at me for a few beats as if she were trying to see into my soul to determine if I was telling the truth or planning on pulling my bongos back out as soon as she turned her back. I did my best to look wholesome and silent. Finally she gave a stiff nod and marched back to her desk.

"She gives librarians a bad name," I whispered to Mandy. "I've got to go. Thanks again."

"You're welcome."

"I mean it. You've gone well above and beyond the librarian code to help those in information need. You've been a huge help to me."

"One of these days, maybe you'll be able to return the favor."

"Say the word, whatever you need."

"I'll keep that in mind." Mandy gave me a strange smile and slipped through the open door to the back.

Chapter 39

I didn't want to wait for a ride, so I decided to walk home. I was a few blocks away when I realized I'd left my phone at the library. I debated leaving it but figured I might need it for my plan. I almost didn't mind all the walking; it was one of those perfect late fall days. For a change it wasn't raining. The sun was shining and the leaves were blowing around, streaks of red and gold.

The cranky librarian was setting a pumpkin down on the stoop to the building. I gave her a smile as I walked past. She didn't look too thrilled to see me. I was willing to bet she thought visiting once a day was plenty. I looked behind the circulation desk and then up and down the aisles, but I didn't see Mandy. I grabbed my phone off the table.

"Can I help you find something?" the librarian asked.

"Um, no. I just forgot my phone. Will you tell the other librarian I'll stop by tomorrow?"

"Other librarian? There's no other librarian. I'm the only one."

Was she trying to make some sort of joke? "You're the only librarian," I repeated. She nodded. I walked past her to the wall of photos behind the low magazine racks. I pointed to a picture of Mandy where she was sitting surrounded by a circle of young kids, all holding up picture books. There was a tag on the picture that said *Nairne Island Young Readers Program*.

"What about her?" I asked. "She looks pretty librarian to me."

"You mean Mandy?" She took a step back. "Mandy's gone."

"Gone? Where did she go?"

"She's been missing for years. She and her sister were the girls who disappeared"—she paused—"up at your house twenty years ago."

Every bone in my body turned to liquid and I slumped to the floor. The blood rushed out of my head and I felt a clammy sweat break out on my forehead. The librarian rushed over and bent down.

"Are you okay? Put your head between your knees." She pressed my head down.

"Mandy's dead."

"Well, no one knows for sure. She and her sister went missing, but I knew their family and there's no way either of those girls would leave their mom and dad without saying something. Not after all this time. My best guess is some sort of accident happened."

Not some sort of accident. I knew exactly what kind of accident. She'd told me. My breathing was low and shallow. Things started clicking into place. I thought of all the dirty looks the librarian had always been giving me. No wonder I was disturbing the library patrons. I must have looked like I was chattering away all by myself in the stacks. Mandy hadn't been there. The only person anyone would have seen was me.

"I have to go." I pushed myself up. The room spun for a moment before things began to steady.

"Why don't you wait here and I'll call your mom to come get you?"

"No, I'm okay." I wasn't okay, but there was no way I was waiting another second. I pushed past the librarian and hurried down the steps. I started walking fast and then broke into a run.

Sweat was pouring off me when I finally got to the driveway. I didn't even stop to put a Band-Aid on the blisters that had sprung up on my run home. I ran into the kitchen and yanked out the drawers, looking for something that would work. I pulled out the meat mallet.

I ran back out of the house. I wasn't sure if I'd be able to find it. The wind was starting to pick up and leaves were blowing around. I followed the tree line along the south side of the house.

I was sure it was there, but I couldn't find it. I broke through the trees and faced the cliff. I must have missed it. I turned around and walked back slower, forcing myself to scan the ground. Nothing. I turned around in a full circle. I felt like screaming in frustration.

I forced myself to close my eyes and slow my breathing down. It would have been dark. It was night when they were here. From here they should have been able to see the house. I opened my eyes and let them skim across the side of the house. The largest bank of windows were those that belonged to Dick's office. It might have been his dad's office then. Twenty years ago Dick would have been college age, but he would have been plenty old enough to do what Mandy described. If the lights had been on in the house, it would have been the brightest point in the night.

The leaves crunched under my feet. I closed my eyes and tried to will myself back to that night. I imagined myself walking through the trees with my sister. We would have been scared, but sort of excited, too. It was an adventure. We would have been holding hands. I let my right hand drop as if I were leading someone behind me. We would have wanted to get closer to see if we could peek in the window. I took a few more steps forward. Then I felt it.

The ground was just a bit higher under my foot. I scraped my foot, clearing away the pine needles and blanket of leaves. The leaves were dry on top, but the bottom layer was still wet from the night before, and they stuck like glue to the wood. I dropped down to my knees and used my hands to clear the rest of the leaves away. The well. I gave the wood a shove, but it didn't move. There were four planks across and they were nailed down to a wooden frame. I pulled out the meat mallet and began whacking at it.

The wood was harder than it looked. I must have pounded on it for at least twenty minutes. My shoulder muscles were screaming every time I lifted the mallet, and blisters were covering my palms. I was panting and sweating from the effort. I was going to have to find something else to break through the wood. There was an axe in the garage. I gave one more whack and a piece of wood cracked off the corner. I shoved my hands in the hole and began to pull the plank back. For a beat nothing happened, but then I could feel the nails starting to give. I kept pulling, grunting. Splinters of wood were cutting into my palms and I could feel them slicing open the blisters. There was a sting of pain as the salt from my sweat trickled into the open wounds.

With a loud crack the wood finally gave way, and I fell back onto my butt, holding the plank in both hands. I tossed it to the side and crawled closer to the hole. It was still too dark. I grabbed ahold of another plank and pulled it back, letting the late-afternoon sun crawl down into the well. At first there was nothing, but then I saw it, a flash of white. A skull. My hands were shaking. I panned around again and saw more bones. There was a glint, and although I couldn't be certain, I was pretty sure it was the heart-shaped locket I'd seen on Mandy's neck.

I lay in the mud, my face pressed against the worn wood, looking through the hole.

"Mandy," I whispered. "I found you."

There was no answer. Not a sound except the wind filtering through the branches above.

"I'm going to make sure you get home, okay?"

I rolled over so that I was looking up. I could see the trees waving back and forth and a corner of the roof of the house. My hands were bleeding and I was filthy. Mandy had done me one more favor. This was going to make my plan perfect. If I called the police, the bodies weren't enough to convict Dick. He could act as if he had no idea they were there. However, if he tried to hide them again, it would be an admission of guilt. It was just the proof I needed.

Chapter 40

I stood in the attic looking at myself in the floor to ceiling mirror. I was wearing the gown that had belonged to Dick's mom. All the glass beading on the dress made it weigh more than I had expected. I'd already brushed the black mousse through my hair to tint it as dark as possible and done my best to pile it in a bun on top of my head. I rooted through my mom's jewelry box and dug out one of the giant brooches that Dick had given her that used to belong to his mom. I pulled a couple of Beanie Babies out of the toy chest and shoved them into my bra to fill out the dress and give myself that steel bustline. I shifted the kitten and the bear until they were level. Better boobs through beanie toys, no surgery required.

I'd already prepared everything downstairs. I'd broken into Dick's office, which wasn't as hard as it looked, because it turns out that every room in the place had the same lock and used the same two-prong skeleton key. I'd unscrewed all the lightbulbs except the one in the desk lamp. Directly under the lamp, I'd placed the two documents and used old Scrabble tiles to spell out the words I KNOW WHAT YOU DID. THE OTHERS WILL BE FOUND. HIDE THEM BEFORE YOU LOSE EVERYTHING. My plan was that Dick would be so scared by the ghostly appearance of his mom and the warning that he would be found out that he would rush to move the bodies. I'd be there, ready to take a picture.

I'd called my mom on my cell and told her I was staying in town to have dinner with my friend when, in reality, I was already upstairs. I had refused to tell Nate what I was up to, but did get him to agree to have his phone on in case I needed him. I looked at my watch. It was time. I lifted the skirt of the dress so I could walk, and slipped down the stairs. I paused in the foyer; I could hear the clink of dishes as they finished up dinner. If Dick stuck to his schedule, and he was nothing if not anal retentive, he would go to his office to check his email.

I slid open the library window and climbed out. The wind was picking up. Even though it was only October, the sun was already down and the night was pitch black. My feet squished through the damp grass as I walked around the house. I shivered. It was colder than I'd expected. I stood outside Dick's office and waited.

Just when I was sure it wasn't going to work for some reason, he showed up. Through the window I could hear the click of

Dick's door and could just make out his shadow. He stood in the doorway clicking the light switch up and down. He took a few steps forward toward the desk. That's when he realized there was something there. Dick picked up the papers and looked them over. I couldn't tell for sure, but it looked like his hands were shaking. He picked up one of the Scrabble tiles and flipped it over, rubbing it like he thought a genie might appear.

I took a deep breath and stepped in front of the window, being sure to stay back far enough that he shouldn't be able to make out my face but would still see my figure. Dick must have seen a flash of movement, because he looked up immediately. The outfit must have had the desired effect, because he instantly stepped back, bumping into the bookshelves behind him. His eyes were open wide and his head shook back and forth. I raised my arm slowly so that I was pointing at him through the glass.

I saw his mouth moving, and I was pretty sure I could make out the word "mommy." He called his mom "mommy"? Ew. And he thought I needed therapy? I shook my head slowly back and forth, my finger pinning him in place.

CRACK. A flash of lightning lit up the entire night sky like a thousand fluorescent lights. I jumped back away from the window before Dick could see me. The skies opened up and the rain dumped down. I was instantly soaked to the skin.

Dick strode toward the window. I picked up the dress and started to run back toward the well. There was a loud boom of thunder, and then I heard the office window slam open.

I tore around the corner of the house, my feet nearly sliding out from under me. The yard was already turning to mud. I crouched underneath one of the trees and held my phone ready to take a photo.

I almost screamed when I saw Dick. He came running around the side of the house holding an axe and a flashlight. He stopped short when he saw that there were already boards broken off the well cover. He used the axe to whack away at the remaining board. Dick looked into the well and cursed. I took a few quick photos with my phone. There was no flash, and I prayed they would show up in the dim light.

Just then my phone rang. Anita's number flashed on the display. I dropped it in the muck and scrambled to pick it up. Dick's head whipped around. Oh shit. I scrambled back but he had already spotted me. He shot forward and grabbed me.

"You." Dick's nostrils were flaring in and out, and the vein on his forehead was bulging.

"Let go of me." I tried to pull my arm back, but Dick had it in a vise grip. My eyes started to burn. I wiped my face and realized the black hair tint was running down my face. My heart was beating a thousand beats a second. The beads on the dress were drilling into my arm where he was holding me.

"I should have known," Dick snarled.

"You killed them. You stole money from your daughter, and when your wife found out and wanted a divorce, you killed them both."

"Is that what you think?"

"That's what I know."

"I didn't kill them. We fought and Sylvie stormed off on the boat. Evie fell off the deck because she was screwing around. That wasn't my fault. The fact that the water was too cold for them and Sylvie couldn't pull her out, that isn't my fault either. None of it was my fault."

"You saw what happened." My mouth fell open. "You must have watched them through the telescope in the library. You saw the whole thing. You could have called for help."

"By the time anyone got out there, they would have been already dead. There wasn't anything anyone could do."

"You don't know that. If you had called for help, at the very least they would have found Evelyn's body."

"Who cares? She didn't know who she was half the time. You think it matters where her body is?"

I pictured the figure of Evie in my room, her mouth open in a scream. "I think it does matter. I think she knew you left her out there."

"You know nothing," Dick spat.

My mind spun around. I thought about Nate talking about his mom and how she would do anything to protect Evie. "Why weren't there any life jackets on board?"

Dick's mouth twitched.

"You took the life jackets off the boat."

"If she cared so much, she should have checked before she

went out." Dick shrugged. "She thought she was so perfect all the time, but even the perfect Sylvia made mistakes. Evelyn wouldn't have died if she had been wearing a life jacket. Sylvia was in such a hurry to get away from me that she didn't make any safety checks. If there is anyone to blame it's her."

"Was my mom involved?"

Dick laughed. "No. But when I called the law firm, your mom was all too happy to give me information about what Sylvia was up to. *She* hit on me, you know. You should have seen her flashing some cleavage and expressing how sorry she was to tell me my wife was planning to leave me. Then when they died she could hardly believe her luck. She didn't care my wife and daughter were barely dead. We cooked up the online story so you wouldn't realize how easy your mom is."

"You're a dick. What about them?" I motioned to the well. "Do you have an explanation for them, too?"

"They had no right to be on this property, but their family still could have sued us because the well cover was rotted. Our family could have lost everything because they were nosy."

"So you left them there to die."

"I left them with the consequences of their actions. Why should my family or I suffer because of their stupidity? How did you even find them?"

"That doesn't matter. You can't hide them anymore," I said. I wanted to spit in his face for what he had done to Mandy.

Dick's face broke into a smile. He pulled me closer. I could smell his breath. "No one is going to know."

"You can't keep me from telling." I tried to keep from shaking. I didn't want him to know how scared I was. His nose was twitching like he could smell the fear and he liked it. "You can call me crazy all you want now, but people are going to listen to me. They're going to believe me when they see this."

"No one will believe you if you never have a chance to open your big mouth."

I looked down. Dick was still holding the axe. His hand was clenching the handle like it was a lifeline. "I've already told. People know," I lied.

Dick laughed. "If you told anyone, you wouldn't be standing out here in my mother's dress trying to collect clues. You haven't told anyone and you're not going to." Dick began dragging me toward the back of the house, near the cliff. I put my feet down and tried to hold myself in place, but between the mud and Dick's strength, he wasn't having any trouble moving me along. "This is your own fault. I would have been willing to get along with you, but you never were happy to leave well enough alone. I hope you're happy. This is going to break your mother's heart."

"What? That she's married to a psycho?" I kept yanking on my arm, trying to get free.

Dick stopped. We were standing on the back patio. The rain bounced off the stone tiles, hitting me on the legs. "She's going to be so upset that you killed yourself. I hope she doesn't blame herself. She should have recognized how troubled you really were. I told her that residential care might be your best bet, but she didn't want to send you away. It's her fault for dragging her feet on making a decision. Your body being found in my mother's dress will really cement the fact that you've been much more unwell than we imagined. I saw you out here and tried to stop you." Dick shook his head sadly. "I'll be devastated, of course."

I screamed. The sound blew back to sea. There was no way anyone in the house would hear me. I started to cry.

"Don't worry. I don't think it will hurt much. I hear the shock of the fall stops your heart before you hit the ground." Dick pulled me closer to the edge. He was going to throw me off. He dropped the axe so that he could grab me with both hands. My body went ice-cold. I was going to die.

I dug at his face, scratching him. He might kill me, but I was going to do everything I could to make sure he would get caught. The scratches would be hard to explain. There might even be DNA under my fingernails. I wouldn't be there to see it, but Dick was going to pay. I felt my phone fall from my pocket and off the cliff. The pictures were gone. I stared him right in the eye and spit.

"Let her go!"

Dick and I both turned around to see Nate. He was looking at his dad with disgust and rage.

"Get back in the house. You're not a part of this."

"I am a part of it. I love her."

"This is more important than a case of puppy love. She'll ruin everything. Think about your family."

"Let her go."

"Go inside. I'll take care of this. Taking care of this family is always up to me."

"And taking care of my family is up to *me*. You step away from her right now." My mom's voice was cold, and she was holding the axe Dick had dropped. There was no shaking of her arms or hesitation in her voice. "Let go of my daughter or I'll make you let go."

Dick let go of my arm and I stepped quickly back from the edge. Nate hugged me close. We stood next to my mom.

"I've done everything for this family," Dick spit out.

The sound of police sirens cut through the night. They were racing up the driveway.

"You've done dick," I said.

"You have to understand," he said, looking at my mom. "She's sick. I found her out here raving about all sorts of crazy things. She wanted to throw herself off the cliff. We have to stick together as a family. We have to get her help."

"You can tell your story to the police," my mom said. "They might be interested in what you have to say. I'm done listening."

I could see flashlight beams bouncing around the side of the house. My mom dropped the axe. Nate pulled me closer. Dick started to cry, but like my mom, I was done listening.

Chapter 41

Nate went to the bathroom to get an old towel to rub the dye off my face. I stood at the edge of my bed. I was exhausted. I'd stripped off the dress and pulled on some sweats. I held the dress out and looked it over. The sleeve was torn and the beads were falling off. There were splotches of black hair tint on the front. It would never be the same.

"I can try and get it dry-cleaned," I mumbled when he walked back into the room.

Nate plopped onto the bed and pulled me down so I was sitting between his legs. He rubbed my face with a corner of the towel. "I don't care about the stupid dress."

"What do you think is going to happen?" After the police arrived, we'd all gone back inside. They had separated all of us and taken everyone's statement. I'd led one of the officer's back outside to the well. Her eyes grew wide when she flashed her light down and saw the bones. She'd whispered into her shoulder walkie-talkie. She sent someone down the trail to the beach to see if they could find my phone. By the time we went back inside, Dick was in handcuffs.

At first I wasn't sure how the police had gotten there so quickly. When he couldn't find me in the house, Nate had decided to sneak out to look for me. My mom discovered Nate sneaking out of the library and they had fought. Anita had called her an hour before and told her she was worried about me. My mom assumed Nate and I were up to something, maybe planning to run away before my appointment in Seattle. Dick had warned her that I might need to be forcibly taken into care. She'd called Dr. Mike and the police to come out to the house.

Once we had come inside with the police, my mom wouldn't let go of my hand. She repeated over and over how sorry she was. She kept crying, and eventually Dr. Mike arranged for Dr. Wilson to come out and give her a shot of something. It seemed like we would have to keep telling our stories over and over, but finally they took Dick away and told us they would be back in the morning. I didn't tell them everything. I didn't tell them about Mandy. I let them think I'd found the bodies when I tripped over the well cover.

"I don't know what's going to happen." Nate sighed. "For the sisters it will be a murder charge. Not getting them help is the same as having pushed them down that well. With my mom and sister, I'm not sure what the charges will be. He just watched them die. In some ways it's almost worse than if he had killed them. At least then it would have been—what do they call it?—a crime of passion. Watching them die just feels like he couldn't be bothered."

"I'm sorry."

"He took the life jackets hoping something would happen. He couldn't stand the idea of anyone, not even his family, coming in between him and what he wanted. It's always been about this stupid house. Who does that? Who sits back and watches his wife and daughter die and can't even be bothered to pick up the phone?"

"Your dad's sick."

"I always sorta knew he wasn't right, you know. People say all the time that they don't think a parent loves them, but with him I knew it was true. He never cared about me; he cared about what I could do for him." He sighed again. "I feel bad for my mom. She would have done anything for Evie. Going out on the boat was what she always did when she was stressed. She would have known she shouldn't jump into the water when Evie fell, that it was too cold. That time of year, you'd have only a few minutes in the water before hypothermia would set in, but she never could sit by. She had to try to save her."

"She was brave."

"Sounds like someone else I know."

I turned around so I could see his face. "You mean me?"

"What you did was either brave or stupid."

"Your dad wasn't supposed to discover I was behind it. He was supposed to think it was the ghost of his mom and then rush out to cover things up so I could get a picture of it. Then we would have taken our proof and gone to the police. It was a good plan."

"It was a plan," he agreed. "I'm not sure it was a good one."

I mock punched him in the shoulder. "If we'd gone to the police, they never would have believed us. Your dad needed something to make him confess, something supernatural."

"You figured there weren't enough ghosts in this house? You had to make your own?"

"So now you believe me that there was a ghost?" I asked, seizing on the point.

"Maybe."

"I think your sister knew what happened. That he left her out there. I think that's why she came back."

"Maybe."

I hated how vague boys could be. I glanced around the room. I'd wondered if Evie would show up when I was having the showdown with her dad, but there had been nothing. Not a blowing curtain or even a pile of seashells. Maybe she didn't need to hear her dad confess; maybe it was enough that someone was listening for her and that the truth would come out.

"You still think with everything that happened, the ghost could have been my subconscious?"

"Don't get touchy. I'm not saying it like there's something

wrong with you. I'm saying it's a possibility. Your brain could have pieced things together and then used the idea of a ghost as a way to make sense of things."

"Fine, it's a possibility." I snorted to give a sense of what I thought of his possibility.

Nate rubbed his face. "I don't want to think about this any more tonight. There will be plenty to sort out tomorrow. I'm guessing our parents are going to get a divorce."

"I guess that takes care of that whole stepbrother, stepsister issue."

"Wash the rest of that stuff out of your hair," Nate said, giving me a soft shove toward the bathroom.

I bent over the sink, letting the warm water rinse through my hair. The swirl of dark tint went down the drain, growing lighter and lighter until the water ran clear and my hair was back to its normal light brown. I pulled a fresh towel off the rack and rubbed my hair dry.

"I take it you don't like me with black hair," I said, leaning against the bathroom doorjamb.

"You dressed like my grandma is not a turn-on."

"I took the dress off."

"That's a turn-on." He held out his hand.

I walked over and took it. He pulled me down onto the bed. He curled up behind me so that we were perfectly spooned. I could feel the heat of his body through our clothes. He nuzzled my neck; his soft kisses made me shiver.

"Still cold?" he whispered into my hair.

"Just a bit." I pressed my body back against his. "What do you think is going to happen with the house?"

"I don't care." His hands found the gap between my sweatshirt and yoga pants. His hands felt hot against my skin as he traced the line of my ribs. "With everything that's happened, I just want to be with you. I have no idea what's going to happen tomorrow. I don't even want to think about it. The only thing I know for sure is that this is where I belong. The house isn't important; it's who you share it with that matters."

I felt my breath quicken. I pulled his arm around me. I opened my eyes. There was still a pile of seashells on the table by my bed. I could feel his breath on my neck. I reached out and pulled the chain for my light. I could hear the rain outside, the plink of raindrops as they blew against the window. In the distance there was a low rumble of thunder. There was enough light coming from outside to see the shape of the furniture in the room. On the bookshelf I could just make out Mr. Stripes.

Then he winked. My breath stopped. I waited to see if it would happen again. I told myself it could have been a trick of the light, but I decided that it was Evelyn giving me her sign of approval.

I rolled over so I was facing Nate. He ran his thumb along the side of my face. I wrapped my arms around him, closed my eyes, and forgot the rest of the world.

Acknowledgments

The very first thanks go to you for reading this book. Without you, I'm left feeling like I'm talking to myself. A writer without a reader is a lonely thing. Special thanks to those of you who have taken the time to write to say you've enjoyed the books. For those of you who have told your friends to read my books, you're my hero.

I've had a longstanding love for librarians, English teachers, and booksellers. For all of you who have been supportive and shared my books with others—thank you. A special call out to the amazing people at Kidsbooks in North Vancouver. I would love your store even if it weren't right next to a cupcake store. (But it is darn convenient.)

A book may be written alone, but publishing takes a whole team. The team at Simon Pulse is amazing. My editor, Anica Mrose Rissi, is a writer's dream. For all the times she's cheered me on and talked me down off a ledge—thank you. I feel fortunate to call you both my editor and my friend. Cara Petrus and Jessica Handelman design covers that make me squeal, and I owe all the marketing and sales people a big kiss for all their support. My agent, Rachel Vater, has been my #1 cheerleader from day one. I'm so glad to still be working with her.

As always I have to thank my family and friends. Special thanks to Alison Pritchard, Serena Robar, Carol Mason, Robyn Harding, Brooke Chapman, Laura Sullivan, Jamie Hillegonds, Joanne Levy, everyone connected to The Debutante Ball, and Jen Lancaster.

To my dogs, who keep me in line, bark-bark, woof.

Sadie wanted to change her life,
but she wasn't prepared to have it flipped upside down.

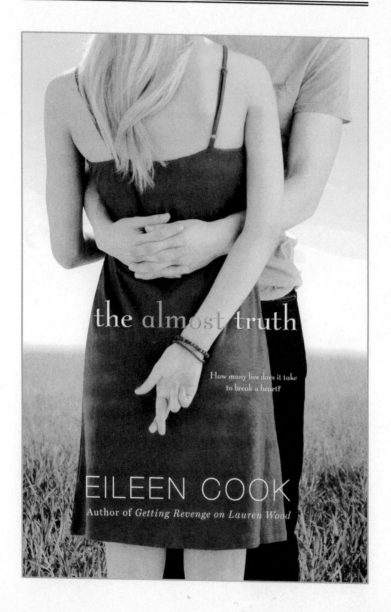

the almost truth

How many lies does it take
to break a heart?

EILEEN COOK

Author of *Getting Revenge on Lauren Wood*

From *The Almost Truth*

Y̲ou know it isn't going to be a good day when you have to choose between food and proper hygiene.

"Can you take the milk off the bill?" I asked the cashier. My cell phone began to ring. I dug around in my bag for it.

"You don't want it anymore?" The cashier tapped her impossibly long fingernails on the register with one eyebrow raised.

"That's right. I don't want the milk," I repeated. This wasn't true. I wanted the milk. Eating dry cereal for a week was going to suck. Not to mention having so little dairy in my diet that I would likely end up with a raging case of osteoarthritis when I was old. But until my mom got paid on Friday, there were limited funds in the house, and there's no way I was going without deodorant. I finally found my phone buried at the very bottom of my bag and yanked it out.

"Sadie, it's Brendan." I didn't need him to tell me his name. Brendan has this habit of yelling into his cell as if it were a tin can on a string.

"Hey," I said. I looked at the new total on the register. *Shit.* "Can you take the toothpaste off too?" We'd have to squeeze a few more days out of the old tube. Now in addition to having brittle bones, I could be toothless. My future was looking brighter and brighter all the time.

The woman in line behind me gave an exasperated sigh. Screw her. She was probably one of those people who always makes you wait while they count out the exact change from their Coach wallet. I turned around. Great, it was Rebecca Samson and her mom. Their cart was piled high with groceries, including that expensive cheese made by yaks that costs something like twenty dollars for an ounce.

"Gosh, Sadie, do you need to borrow a couple dollars?" Rebecca asked, fighting to keep a smirk off her face. Her mom might have also been trying to smirk, but her face was so Botoxed she was incapable of expression.

"Hey! Is that Blow Job Becky I hear? What are you doing hanging with the cheerleader from hell?" Brendan bellowed. His voice carried out of my phone like he was on speaker. Rebecca's face froze as hard as her mother's.

"The total's twenty-two fifteen. How does that work for you?" The cashier tapped her fingernails again.

"Hang on, I'm at the store," I said to Brendan. I plunked my phone down on the conveyor belt and pulled some cash out of my bag. I made sure to spread the two twenty-dollar bills out in a fan shape so they could be clearly seen by the cashier and Blow Job Becky, too.

The cashier snapped her gum when she saw the money. No doubt she wondered why I had nickeled and dimed my bill when I had forty bucks. She handed over my change. I palmed the ten-dollar bill she gave me and, with my thumbnail, pulled a folded five-dollar bill from under my watchband. I made a show of counting the bills. "I'm sorry. I think you didn't give me enough change." I held out the two fives, a couple ones, and eighty-five cents.

The cashier screwed up her face. "I swore I gave you a ten. Sorry." She pulled another five out of the drawer and handed it to me.

"No problem." I tucked the money into my bag and took the groceries from her. An extra five bucks was going to come in handy. I could use it to buy milk, but I had more immediate needs than staving off osteoarthritis. I smiled at Rebecca and her Botoxed mom and stepped outside. As soon as the automatic doors closed behind me, it felt like I was slapped in the face with the hot, wet air. It might sound good in theory, but summer sort of sucks unless you can spend it sitting by the ocean with a fruity drink. Spending it in a parking lot with your T-shirt damp and sticking to you isn't that much fun.

"Sorry about that, you caught me in the middle of something,"

I said into the phone. I leaned against the warm cinder-block wall. A small kid was standing near me, staring at the pony ride next to the row of gum-ball machines. I tried to ignore him, but he looked like someone had shot his puppy. I sighed and handed him a quarter. He broke into a smile and climbed up on the mechanical horse, leaned forward, and fed the machine the coin. Ah, when joy could be purchased for less than a buck.

"Are you still running that wrong change con for five bucks?" Brendan said. "I keep telling you to up the ante. If you cashed in a hundred-dollar bill, you could easily clear twenty bucks."

"Twenty bucks is more likely to get noticed," I pointed out. "Not to mention if I start flashing hundred-dollar bills around town, that's going to seem weird."

"So you're doing the small con just to be careful? Are you trying to tell me it has nothing to do with the fact that if the short is less than five dollars then the cashier doesn't have to pay it out of their own pocket?"

I dragged my sneaker on the cement. "Being a cashier at the Save-on-Food Mart is punishment enough. She doesn't need to cover me."

Brendan laughed. "Your ethics are getting in the way of the big score, but hey, it's your choice. What are you up to tonight? I was thinking we could go over to Seattle and grab dinner."

I snorted, knowing full well Brendan's idea of grabbing dinner. "You buying or is the restaurant?" I asked.

"Now why in the world would I pay?" Brendan wasn't teasing.

He actually was incapable of understanding why he should have to pay for anything when he was clever enough to steal it without getting caught.

"While stealing a meal with you sounds like an attractive option, I'm going to have to say no."

"For a con artist you have a highly overinflated sense of morals," Brendan said. "Especially when dinner is on the line. We could go for Japanese if you want."

"Don't call me that. Besides, you hate Japanese."

"Yet another good reason I shouldn't have to pay for it."

I rolled my eyes. If you wanted to get technical about it, I *was* a con artist. I'd learned the tricks of the trade from my dad. Then I taught what I knew to Brendan, who happened to have some sort of freakish natural ability in the area. He was like a con genius savant. However, unlike Brendan, who just loved getting away with something, I preferred to see it as a means to an end, an end that was finally coming to a close. "I can't go to dinner, I've got stuff to do tonight."

"Like what?"

Most people would take a polite brush off and move on. Brendan was not most people. "I have stuff to get ready for school."

"You're not going away to college for months. C'mon, a night in the city would be fun."

I knew down to the exact day (sixty-four, counting today) how soon I would be leaving Bowton Island for college. If I were better at math, I would be counting down the hours in my head. "I want to do some packing," I said. The truth was, it wouldn't take me that long to pack. My bedroom was the size of a closet. Even if I took the time to fold each item of my clothing into a tiny origami crane, there'd be no need to start now. The problem was spending time with Brendan felt weird lately. We'd known each other since we were kids, and on an island where 90 percent of the residents measured their wealth in terms of millions, and those of us in the remaining 10 percent measured it by having enough to buy groceries, we were automatic allies. Brendan had been my best friend as long as I could remember.

Brendan was the one who'd realized that the pranks I'd taught him could be used to pull cons to raise cash. He helped me figure out what I needed to do to escape my life. I would always owe him for that. The problem was, he didn't want me to leave. Or at least he didn't want me to leave without him, but where I was going there would be no room for him. I was planning to make over my entire life, and that meant leaving the old me behind.

Then there was the uncomfortable realization that Brendan maybe wasn't thinking of me as just his best friend anymore. There'd been a few awkward moments where I'd caught him staring at me, and at graduation I'd thought he might try to kiss me. And not in a "wow, we're great friends and we survived high school" kind of way.

"Maybe we could do it another time?" I asked.

"Fine, but you can't blow me off forever," Brendan grumped.

"I'm not blowing you off. I'm tired, that's all."

"Then get some sleep and we'll do tomorrow night. No excuses." Brendan clicked off before I could say anything else.

I tossed my cell back into my bag. I pulled out the ten-dollar bill I'd dropped in there after palming it and stuck it in my wallet. Taking a five at a time wasn't adding up fast, but combined with the money from my part-time job at the hotel, it did add up. Brendan could tease me if he wanted, but I knew that while larger cons might pay off better, they also came with much bigger risks. My dad was a living, breathing example of that. For as long as I could remember, he had been in jail more often than he'd been out. I suspected the correctional officers knew him better than I did. One year when he was on probation, they sent him a birthday card.

For Brendan, the point was the con, not the cash. As soon as the money came in, it went right back out. I'd been stockpiling mine. In three and a half weeks I would put most of it down to hold my place at Berkeley. I was going to college, and I planned to leave all of this behind me.

The doors to the grocery swooshed open and Rebecca and her mom came out. Her mom pushed their cart past me as if I didn't even exist. I suspected she saw me like the help, best ignored unless she needed something. Rebecca glanced over at my Old Navy T-shirt and my cutoff shorts. Somehow she managed to look cool and unphased by the heat. It was like being really rich also made her immune to humidity and the need to sweat.

"Nice outfit," she said, her smirk in full force.

"Aw, that would hurt my feelings if I cared about your opinion," I said. This was a concept Rebecca had never fully grasped. She felt everyone should want her love and approval. She was also open to ass kissing. It really chafed her fanny that I didn't care what she thought of me. It must have made her job as the popular mean girl so much less enjoyable when what she said didn't bother me. She was also apparently unaware of the fact that high school was now over, making her the queen bee of nothing. I noticed a glint of silver on her perfectly pressed polo shirt. "Is that your cheerleading pin?" I asked.

Rebecca fingered the silver megaphone. "It's my captain's pin."

I couldn't decide if it was merely sad or full-on pathetic that she was still wearing it postgraduation. Rebecca was going to grow up to be one of those overly skinny women who hang out at the country club bitching about how their husbands are never around, how their maids don't scrub the toilets to their satisfaction, and how high school was the best time of their lives. Personally, I was planning on my life getting better from this point forward.

I picked up my bag of groceries. "You have a good rest of the summer," I called over my shoulder at her as I walked away. Being nice to Rebecca would screw with her head more than any sarcastic comeback. I tucked my bag into the basket attached to the back of my scooter. Rebecca might mock my secondhand clothes and Brendan might make fun of my five-dollar cons, but in sixty-four days none of it would matter.

Unlike Rebecca, I didn't plan to look back on high school with fondness. I didn't plan to look back on it at all.

EILEEN COOK spent most of her teen years wishing she were someone else or somewhere else, which is great training for a writer. When she was unable to find any job postings for world-famous author, she went to Michigan State University and became a counselor so she could at least afford her book-buying habit. But real people have real problems, so she returned to writing because she likes having the ability to control the ending. Which is much harder with humans.

You can read more about Eileen, her books, and the things that strike her as funny at eileencook.com. Eileen lives in Vancouver with her husband and dogs, and no longer wishes to be anyone or anywhere else.

Love. Heartbreak.
Friendship. Trust.

Fall head over heels for
Terra Elan McVoy.

Girls you like. Emotions you know. Outcomes that make you think.

ALL BY
DEBCALETTI